Designed FOR *You*

Designed for You
MARCIA KING-GAMBLE

ARABESQUE®

DESIGNED FOR YOU

An Arabesque novel

ISBN 1-58314-620-2

© 2006 by Marcia King-Gamble

www.kimanipress.com

Printed in U.S.A.

Dedication

I would be remiss if I did not thank
George Johnston (Mike), urban designer
extraordinaire, for putting himself at my disposal.
His helpful and insightful comments saved me
from doing extensive research. If you're ever
looking for a talented urban designer,
www.JTPhome.com is the place.

Dear Reader,

When I first started writing *Designed for You,* I had this crazy notion that an architect and an urban designer were one and the same.

Not so. A friend who was an urban designer soon set me straight. While both parties are visionaries, the urban designer creates people friendly urban communities where real people live.

You may have heard of *gentrification.* Usually that means the transformation of spaces or communities that were at one time labeled unsafe wastelands. Take, for example, South Beach in Florida, Harlem in New York and Pasadena in California. This is where your urban designer's talents are showcased.

Can you imagine having the opportunity to put your unique stamp on a place?

When I wrote *Designed for You,* I wanted to introduce you to a new and worthy career, one in which your can mastermind change. I'd also hoped to show you that love is possible even between adversaries like Jana and Reese. Hopefully I was successful.

Please e-mail me at mkinggambl@aol.com. Or you may write to me at P.O. Box 25143, Tamarac, FL 33320.

Be sure to include a stamped, self-addressed envelope.

May you find someone uniquely "Designed for You."

Best,

Marcia King-Gamble
www.lovemarcia.com

Chapter 1

"Changes are coming to Lakeview Park," Twyla Lewis announced through the mouthpiece. "We need to take advantage of them."

"What changes?" Jana Davis asked distractedly, balancing the receiver between ear and shoulder, her attention still focused on the file in front of her.

"Come on, Jana," Twyla pleaded. "Let's not look a gift horse in the mouth. Weren't you just saying A Fare to Remember could use more business?"

"Yes, I was. But are we ready to take on some swanky affair with lots of important people complaining about every detail?"

"Sure we are. The more high profile the affair, the better. I vote we throw our hat in the ring."

Twyla—Jana's friend, colleague, and new business partner—rambled on undaunted. "It's not just one event, it's two. One's the groundbreaking luncheon. The other is the dinner dance. We've got two shots to make money and get ourselves some press."

"Is there still ground to be broken in San Diego?" Jana asked, wrinkling her nose.

"I knew you weren't listening, if so you'd be pretty damn mad."

What was Twyla talking about? Jana's mind was focused on Lucy Santana, whose file she'd been reading. The teenager was in trouble.

"Come back to me," Twyla called through the phone's earpiece. "We need to do some brainstorming."

It had been Jana's idea to start A Fare to Remember, their event-planning business. Both had realized that social work barely paid the bills. After tossing around a number of ideas they'd decided on event planning, a business that would require only a minimal outlay of money: just enough to cover fliers and the mailbox they could rent. A website would come later on when they felt flush.

Twyla and Jana balanced each other beautifully. Whereas Twyla was superorganized and had a degree in finance and a second in culinary art, Jana was the creative force, the idea person. It was Jana who had the unique ability to turn the most mundane object into an artistic piece of work. And she could charm the pants off the grouchiest person.

"Where is this event anyway?" Jana asked, her mind still on Lucy Santana and her latest drama.

"In Lakeview Park. I told you that."

Jana still didn't get it. What was this about a ground-breaking and an event in Lakeview Park?

"Why would anyone plan an event in such a seedy venue?" she asked. "The la-de-da crowd isn't going to want to come to the hood."

"Bet you anything they will. They'll want to see and be seen. Besides, there's only so much waterfront property left in the country and those forty-plus acres in the southeast section of San Diego are prime real estate."

"But the park and the surrounding land are owned by the city."

"No it's not. It's privately owned. Now that the lease has expired, it's been bought by a developer and you know what that means."

Finally it sunk in, what Twyla was trying to tell her. Jana's back went up. She clutched the receiver.

"Here we go again," she groused. "And people wonder why crime in black communities is on the increase? Most of our people can't afford a fancy health club. That's one of the reasons this run-down facility works. It certainly is one of the reasons I volunteer my services."

Jana had always acknowledged that Lakeview Park was down at the heels. She fondly referred to it as a worn old shoe that with a little spit and polish might possibly regain its luster. From what Twyla just said, it was about to get a whole new sole. While very much needed, the black community it served would be out. There was no place in the surrounding area that offered free recreational facilities or counseling services to those down-and-out.

Her friend's voice came at her through the earpiece again. "You always said Lakeview had great potential, Jana."

"It does. But I guarantee you the plans are to build fancy town houses and pricey boutiques on that waterfront. The community center will probably be torn down."

Twyla groaned. "Yeah, I suppose, but don't go getting your knickers in a twist yet. Let's stay focused. A Fare to Remember needs to bring in money. Either we jump on the opportunity to cater both affairs or someone else will. Let's take advantage of my contacts and put our bid in."

What Twyla said made sense but it still bothered Jana. She couldn't help worrying about what this change would mean for the neighborhood. In the six months she'd volunteered at the center she'd grown close to the people who came there. She was used to listening to their problems and celebrating their small victories. Now they thought of her as a friend.

As Twyla gabbed on, Jana grew increasingly more uncomfortable. *Lakeview* was the only oasis in the otherwise poverty-stricken environment. Although poorly maintained, young people played on the handball and basketball courts, working off the frustrations of the grueling city life. Despite being unkempt, the hiking and rollerblading paths were frequently used.

Here at the community center, where Jana volunteered, the elderly sipped coffee and played never-ending games of checkers. They sat on the peeling park benches and caught up on gossip, exchanging tall tales about their youth.

The stay-at-home moms loved coming to *Lakeview.* In small armies, they charged through the park, pushing strollers or balancing gurgling babies on their hips. The rusty playground equipment, though not particularly attractive, got a constant workout.

"So I say we go for it," Twyla persisted. "I'll call my contact and let her know we're interested."

"Fine," Jana said, though bile rose in her throat. The minute she and Twyla got off the phone she would verify this information. Ken Gibson, the executive director of the Lakeview Park Community Center, would know. And today was one of the rare times he was actually on the premises.

Tucking an escaping lock of honey-blond hair into a

scarf tied seventies'-fashion, Jana set off to find Ken. On her way she almost ran smack into Lucy Santana.

"Hey, Jana," Lucy chirped. "That skirt rocks. Where did you find it?"

Jana smiled wryly. Lucy's fashion sense pretty much matched her own. Today the precocious teenager wore red footless tights under a black miniskirt.

"The consignment shop on Fifth. You're early for our session, Lucy."

"Yeah, I know. But Drew's playing basketball." Lucy winked at Jana before eyeing her up and down. "You bought that skirt at the vintage place up the street? How come I can never find anything there?"

Jana playfully whacked Lucy's arm. "Maybe you need to make time to rifle through the racks and look for sales. See you in fifteen minutes, hon. And don't be late."

Jana moved on, smiling at how irked her uptight mother would be if she'd heard Lucy referring to the era she'd grown up in as vintage. It was almost impossible to picture the proper Dr. Davis in funky bellbottoms and platform shoes. Nor could Jana picture the stiff woman she referred to as Mother in the colorful gypsy skirts she herself favored. They were as unlike as two people could ever be.

Ken's office door was closed, a sure indication someone was in there with him. Then again maybe he was writing one of his many fund-raising letters. Since there was no one around to ask, Jana knocked on the door.

"Who is it?" Ken Gibson's baritone boomed.

"Jana. If you're busy I can come back."

"We're pretty much wrapped up anyway."

We? The door opened and Jana faced the dark-skinned executive director and a tall, honey-colored man she'd never seen before. The visitor had a sheaf of paper rolled up under one arm. Brown eyes sparkled as he met Jana's gray ones.

"That's quite the outfit," he said.

What was it about her outfit today that made everyone comment? The wide turquoise skirt and her silver jewelry were her tribute to spring. The scarf tied around her head with the fringes hanging down her back was worn for practicality more than style.

Defiantly, Jana cocked her head and narrowed her eyes. The chandelier earrings that touched her shoulders jingled. "Is that a compliment? Am I supposed to say thank you?"

"What do you think?"

Ken looked at them with interest. Seconds went by before he cleared his throat.

"Reese McDonald, this is Jana Davis," he finally offered up. "Jana's a social worker, one of our volunteers."

Reese shook her hand and then held onto it, examining the silver cuff at her wrist. After a decent interval she extricated herself from his grip.

It was fairly apparent Ken wasn't about to share Reese's occupation. Time to take matters into her own hands. Eyeing the rolled-up papers tucked under Reese's arm, Jana asked, "What is it that you do?"

"I'm actually an urban designer," he answered. He was well over six feet and towered above her.

"Why does the center need an architect?"

"Urban designer," he corrected.

Ken, although outwardly flustered by her brassiness, kept his mouth shut. Reese merely looked mildly amused.

"Nice hair color," he said. "Is it natural?"

"Is yours?"

Reese's hair was so dark it contrasted sharply with his creamy skin. His features didn't have the slightest wrinkle and it was hard to tell how old he was. No point in matching wits, Jana decided. Might as well find out as much as she could. Twyla's sources so far had been right, as they usually were. But things were moving faster than either of them had anticipated.

"Do you know what an urban designer does?" Reese McDonald asked as if she was just a tad slow.

Let him think what he would.

"No, suppose you tell me."

"We create visions for how a property should look."

"You mean lack of vision," Jana muttered. "Duh! I should have known!" She stabbed her index finger in the vicinity of his chest, connecting with air. "And you're one of the hired hands retained to make that happen."

Reese's smile appeared even more smug. "I am?" His eyebrows winged upward.

Ken, who appeared to be rendered speechless, looked from one to another, trying to assess if the ribbing was in jest, or if the two were actually going at each other.

"How did you hear the news?" Ken finally asked her. "The plans for Lakeview Park aren't public knowledge."

"Oh yes they are. Word's out on the street. Why haven't you had the decency to tell the people who work here first?"

Jana noticed Ken was having a hard time looking her in the eye. She folded her arms and waited.

"I planned on calling a meeting later today," Ken mumbled. "It's the very reason I came in."

Reese McDonald actually had the grace to look uncomfortable. He quickly shook Ken's hand and nodded at Jana. "I'll leave you two alone. We'll be in touch." With that Reese headed off.

"Well?" Jana asked, unfolding her arms after Reese was out of earshot. "Why weren't we told? How come I had to hear the news elsewhere?"

Ken still couldn't meet her eyes. "Nothing was finalized," he mumbled.

Ken Gibson was the world's biggest wuss. Like most men he would do anything to avoid conflict. He'd probably come in to work on a memo detailing the plans for Lakeview Park. He'd take the easy way out and that would solve the issue of having a meeting. That way no uncomfortable questions would be asked.

Now, by confronting him, Jana had forced his hand. Remembering Lucy Santana was waiting, she flounced off. "Let me know when the meeting starts," she said loudly.

"Sure thing."

Jana turned, tossing over her shoulder: "By the way, that architect…uh, urban designer guy, is a jerk."

Jana was running late as always. Deciding not to use the valet parking, she parked the pickup truck in the first available spot, tossing a handful of change into the meter. Then she hurried toward the Mexican restaurant where she and Twyla had agreed to meet.

Twyla was already seated on the outside patio under an umbrella. From the look of the almost-empty chips-and-salsa dish, she'd been there a while. She was working on an oversized margarita.

Jana flopped down across from her. "Sorry I'm late."

Twyla set down her margarita on the Formica table

and made a wry face. "What's new? You've been late for the twenty-odd years since I've known you." She waved to the waitress. "Bring us two more melon margaritas."

Theirs was a friendship that went way back. Twyla and Jana had actually met the first day of kindergarten when they'd fought over whose turn it was to use the playground swing. With the exception of the four years when they'd gone out of state to college, they'd been practically joined at the hip.

"You were right," Jana said, helping herself to what was left of the chips.

"Right about what?"

"Lakeview Park and its upcoming gentrification."

"You verified that, I take it?"

"Yup. I met one of the architects today. Actually he calls himself an urban designer, quite an obnoxious man. And I confronted our illustrious executive director, with what you told me, forcing him to hold a meeting."

"Mmmmmm, mmmmm, mmmm. Poor Ken. He was probably shaking in his boots."

"Poor Ken nothing. He's got degrees up the ying yang and will easily find himself another cushy job."

Twyla knew Ken well. At one point she'd also volunteered at the center. Now she worked at Mercy Hospital. Between the day job, moonlighting at A Fare to Remember, and her hot new romance, she didn't have a moment to spare. Twyla no longer had the time to volunteer.

"What do we need to do to make sure A Fare to Remember wins the bid?" Jana asked.

"Nothing, darling. It's pretty much a done deal. I mentioned to my contact we'd come in twenty percent below any competitor. In return, we'd expect A Fare to be mentioned in all press releases."

"You're brilliant," Jana said, clinking the oversized margarita glass, which came complete with salted rim, against Twyla's glass. "Hopefully this gig will elevate our status."

Twyla sighed. "And bring money in. We took a beating on that Little League lunch last Sunday. The group still hasn't made their final payment." She eyed Jana's almost-empty glass. "Maybe we should have another margarita and plan strategy?"

"Sure. Why not?"

For the next half an hour, Twyla filled Jana in on the planned events.

"We'll have to go all out and make these events special. This is where your creativity comes into play. The mayor, city council, and the usual hangers-on will be on the guests list as will other notables of San Diego. If we do this right, word will spread and we should be able to pick up a sizeable amount of business."

"It's what A Fare to Remember needs. Business," Jana remarked after draining the last remnants of her margarita. "This is my treat." She signaled to the waitress for the check. "I have an early appointment tomorrow at Planned Parenthood."

Planned Parenthood was where Jana actually worked. The salary left something to be desired, and her parents, both doctors, thought she was crazy. Yet Jana had remained with the family planning organization even after getting her master's. She volunteered two days a week at the Lakeview Park Community Center because it assuaged the guilt she felt for being born into a family of privilege. Perhaps she was fooling herself, but she thought she made a difference. The teenagers she counseled trusted her.

"I have an early meeting tomorrow as well," Twyla said

through a loud yawn. She tucked a stray lock behind one ear and narrowed her eyes at Jana. "What's this architect—I mean, urban designer—like?"

"Tall, light-skinned, arrogant."

Twyla's eyebrows rose. "Black and single?"

"Black, yes. Single, who knows? Who cares?"

Twyla was now standing, gathering her purse. "I do. Why didn't you check out his ring finger, girlfriend?"

Jana rolled her eyes. "Because I don't care whether he's married or not. I told you I didn't like him."

"I might like him, especially if he's single, black and professional. We're in his league. He might be the perfect hookup."

"For you maybe, but not for me. I'm not going to get near some guy who's out to ruin Lakeview Park. This community has embraced me from the very beginning and I can't sell them out." An idea niggled at the back of Jana's mind. "Maybe I'll put together a citizens' group." That produced a smile. She threw her hands in the air, palms up. "Picture this: 'Save Lakeview Park and what it stands for.'"

"You will not."

"I will too."

There was nothing Jana liked better than taking a stand for something she believed in. The community of Lakeview was in danger and needed to be saved.

Chapter 2

Reese McDonald paced the confines of the hotel room that he now called home. He'd accepted the assignment to design the forty acres of Lakeview property, knowing it might easily be a two-year commitment. And that's exactly what interested him. He'd needed to get away from Baltimore and put some painful memories behind him. The challenge of a new development would help take his mind off his woes.

As he peered out of the window, and down on the bay with its bobbing sailboats, his cell phone rang.

"Mr. McDonald, I'm in the lobby," a nasal female voice said the moment he picked up.

"I'll be right down."

Glancing out of the hotel's tinted floor-to-ceiling windows, Reese realized it was a bright, sunny day, perfect weather to go house hunting. Not that he had all day. He planned on heading over to Lakeview Park later and taking a look around.

Jacqueline Jiminez, the realtor who'd been assigned to him by Bruce Rothschild, who was essentially his boss, was mincing around the hotel lobby in too-high heels. She reminded him of a rooster. Reese recognized her because of the photos on her business card and website. How long would she last showing him houses in those killer heels? Her feet were bound to hurt like hell.

"Jackie?" he asked, approaching her. On the phone she'd told him that was the name she preferred.

The realtor turned and looked him over. "I'm Jackie Jiminez," she said.

"Reese McDonald."

Jackie's look of amazement was one he recognized and had grown used to. His lily-white name seemed to throw off a number of people. Jackie Jiminez, who handled corporate relocations for the Rothschilds, was not expecting an African American.

Reese's good manners kicked in. He smiled and extended a hand. We said we'd meet at ten. You're to show me homes and town houses."

Jackie Jiminez was good. She quickly recovered, pumped Reese's hand, and offered a professional smile. "Mr. McDonald, you're in good hands. Have you had breakfast?"

Reese assured her he had.

"In that case let's get started."

Jackie Jiminez was dressed in an expensive designer suit. She minced alongside him, stopping briefly to remove a valet ticket from her purse. And though she was nothing like the throwback at the Lakeview Park Center, something about her confident strut brought to mind the gypsy of the other day.

"It's beautiful weather," Jackie chirped after they'd stepped outside and she'd handed the ticket to an overeager valet.

"Yes, it is."

Reese noted the Lexus as it pulled up. The status car fit the realtor perfectly. Soon they were on their way, driving through perfectly groomed neighborhoods—Jackie must have carefully planned their route.

"Do you have a family?" Jackie asked taking her eyes off the road ahead.

"No."

She glanced at him again. He could tell from her expression she didn't care for his one-word answer.

"I'm thinking maybe a villa or town house would best fit your needs."

"Whatever. But keep in mind I have two dogs in Baltimore. I'll be bringing them here."

The truth was Reese really hadn't given much thought to housing. All he was concerned about was having a place to lay his head. He'd always been something of a workaholic. It had gotten worse now that he had no reason to go home.

"We're heading downtown." If Jackie was upset that he'd snubbed her, she hid it well. "I was thinking a single man might want a little more action than the suburbs would bring. I'm taking you to San Diego's urban neighborhoods."

Reese grunted and gazed out the partially opened window. He sniffed the salt in the crisp spring air, a sure reminder they were surrounded by water.

Jackie continued on with her monologue. She told him all about San Diego being the sixth-largest city in the United States. Then she went on to say that Mission Bay, the East Village, and Little Italy—although three distinctly different neighborhoods—had personalities of their own.

"Any idea where you'd like to start first?" Jackie asked.

"Not a clue. You pick."

They drove through an area called Cortez Hill, supposedly one of the oldest residential areas, and charming to boot. Blooming jacaranda trees lined storybook streets, coating them in picturesque lavender blue.

"Looks pretty pricey," Reese commented, primarily for something to say, and because he felt sorry for Jackie. He'd made no real effort to put her at ease.

"It is. I'm thinking perhaps we should start with the Marina District."

"Why not."

The next four hours went by quickly as Jackie squired him through an assortment of houses and townhomes. Not that he knew what he was looking for, but none of them felt right.

Finally Reese said, "Shall we call it a day? The next time we meet up maybe you could show me neighborhoods that are more diverse. I'd like to see where real people live."

She shot him a look that implied he might be difficult but then covered it with a smile. "Perhaps City Heights is a possibility. It's sort of a melting pot and many areas are being gentrified."

"I'm open."

Reese had already read between the lines. City Heights's colorful demographics made it not the most desirable place to live. But money was money when you worked for the most part on commission and he would make her take him there the next time they were out.

Glancing at his watch, Reese realized it was much later than he'd thought. "Can you step on it?" he asked. "I've got to go to work and I have another commitment."

"You're working on a Saturday?" Jackie's knitted

brows indicated her skepticism. But she did comply with his request and shortly afterward they were back where they'd started.

"What are you going to do about your situation?" Jana asked the belligerent teenager seated across from her.

"It's not my problem," Drew Nelson answered, his stony gaze focused on the cream wall where Jana had hung motivational quotes.

"It *is* your problem, Drew. It takes two people to get pregnant."

Andrew Nelson's brown eyes hardened. This time he met Jana's gaze head-on. "It wasn't like I was in love with her or anything. She kept coming after me. She wouldn't take no for an answer. She offered herself to me. I jumped at that chance."

Jana felt her anger build. This was the boy Lucy Santana was crazy about. Apparently he wasn't crazy about her. But as a professional Jana had to remain impartial. She couldn't say how she really felt, but she could make him think.

"You're responsible for your own actions, Drew," Jana said. "Don't blame this on Lucy. Now the two of you need to decide what you want to do."

"There's no two of us. Lucy and I hooked up. I've been going with Kendra since the beginning of the year."

"Well, Drew, regardless, Lucy is pregnant and you two are going to have to talk about this."

Jana closed the file in front of her, communicating their half hour had ended.

Drew stood, his shoulders hunched. "I suppose I'm going to have to do something. Kendra's going to be damn pissed if she finds out about that girl. She'll have my ass."

Jana wasn't cutting him any slack.

"'That girl's' name is Lucy. And if I were you I'd have that conversation soon. Next Saturday when we meet you can tell me how it went."

Jana watched Drew shuffle out. He had an angry look on his face. His irresponsibility didn't sit well with her.

So far it had been one helluva week and she was burnt. She'd dealt with the Right to Lifers on the sidewalks of Planned Parenthood. They'd not made coming and going easy. The police eventually put an end to the mess when some of the picketers grew disorderly and threatened the lives of several employees.

All in all, it had been an emotionally draining and traumatic experience. Jana had so looked forward to the weekend, even though two hours of her Saturday would be devoted to counseling kids at the Lakeview Park Community Center. Thankfully, Drew Nelson was her last appointment of the day.

Time had passed quickly. Now she would barely be able to race home, take a quick shower, and head to Pacific Beach where Twyla was already setting up for the retirement party. A Fare to Remember had been hired to plan and cater a dinner for twenty-plus guests.

To keep costs down, she and Twyla would both serve and tend bar, and they'd hired Lucy Santana to help out where needed. The troubled teenager's mother had tossed her out on the street, forcing her to live with an aunt. Lucy desperately needed the money.

Quickly shutting the door on her broom closet of an office, Jana took off. She sprinted across the parking lot toward her hot red pickup truck, and then slowed.

A silver Range Rover was parked directly behind her, blocking her in.

"Dammit!" Jana said out loud, then let another expletive rip. She circled the vehicle, shaking her head and muttering.

"It's not like this is a weekday. There are plenty of vacant spots." Now she'd have to waste even more time hunting the inconsiderate person down. Frustrated, she kicked the Rover's bumper. "Jerk!"

"Would that jerk be me?"

The voice was male and came from behind her.

Jana spun around and spotted the tall, light-skinned man loping toward her. Even though he was casually dressed in khaki walking shorts and a polo shirt she recognized him instantly as the urban designer. Besides, he was carrying a set of rolled-up drawings under his arm.

Jana jutted a thumb in the direction of the overpriced vehicle. "You're here on a Saturday?" she asked. "Is that thing yours?"

"Yes, I'm working just like you."

Reese McDonald's sparkling brown eyes assessed her attire. His lips twitched. He clearly found something amusing. "Cute. You do know how to make a fashion statement."

Smart-ass. He was certainly no one to comment, given his prepped-out look. Jana slowly let her gaze roam over him. "As do you. Is that East Coast attire?"

"Yes, we dress a little more conservatively in Baltimore. By the way that wasn't a put-down. At least you have the courage to take a stand. Most kids your age are wearing hiphuggers and baring midriffs."

"The slacks are called low-risers. And I'm not a kid. I'm twenty-six years old."

"You look much younger."

Jana knew she did. Her youthful appearance often worked to her advantage. It helped her to get through to the teenagers she counseled since they thought of her as one of them.

Jana glanced down at the buttercup-yellow capris she'd hastily thrown on. In actuality they were pedal pushers bought at another consignment shop. She'd hurriedly flung on a black oversized T-shirt that in red lettering read: I AM WOMAN, HEAR ME ROAR. Another find from the same store.

The top and bottom had cost her less than five dollars. Even the flip-flops, with the sunflowers partially covering her big toes, cost more. The entire outfit had been put together for less than twenty dollars, and that included the yellow-and-red hobo bag slung over her shoulder.

Jana was suddenly anxious to get away from Reese McDonald. He was starting to make her uncomfortable. "If that Range Rover's yours you'll need to move it," she said.

"You may not want me to."

Reese McDonald's smile was the kind that warmed the stoniest of hearts. He'd probably used it a million times to disarm. Jana was not about to let him get over on her.

"Just please move your truck."

"I can, but you probably don't want me to, not if you want help with that flat."

"What flat?"

Reese pointed to the left back tire. "If you ease up on the hostility, darling, I might even help you change it."

She had no choice. She was already late for the party. "I'm sorry," Jana said. "I guess I overreacted."

Reese had already squatted down and was examining the flat tire. "It was the first thing I noticed when I pulled into the parking lot. I figured somebody would be mighty pissed when they were ready to go home. So I pulled up and raced into the center hoping to find them."

He'd been a Good Samaritan and look where it had gotten him. Jana now had a problem even looking at him.

"I can have that tire changed and you on your way in less than fifteen minutes," Reese said affably. "Do you have a spare?"

"Yes." She showed him where her spare and jack were kept.

Shooting her another devastating smile, Reese set to work. For the first time Jana noticed the dimple in his cheek when he smiled and how his brown eyes changed to an interesting shade of sherry. She supposed most women would think him handsome.

She also knew there would probably be a price to pay for his chivalry, but beggars couldn't be choosers. Reese, true to his word, was almost done replacing the tire.

"You picked up a nail," he said. "You could probably plug the tire and it would save you the expense of an immediate purchase."

Reese had probably taken one look at her clothing and figured she was destitute. Whatever. Let him think what he would. Jana thanked him and prepared to take off. On impulse she added, "I'm late for an appointment or I'd invite you to have a drink."

"Why don't I take a rain check, then?" he answered, surprising her. "Do you have a business card?"

He removed a crisp beige card from his wallet and

handed it to her. Jana was left with no choice but to reciprocate.

Reese glanced at the business card that Planned Parenthood had paid for and made a wry face. "You're a social worker. You like to save people."

"No, I like to help."

So much for being civil. Jana climbed into her truck and slammed the door. The awning in the back bounced up and down. She wound down her window.

"I'm backing out now. Can you move your vehicle out of the way?"

"Aye, aye, madam."

Jana thought she heard Reese mutter, "So much for being a nice guy."

She would bet anything he wasn't.

Chapter 3

"You're late!" Twyla greeted, the moment Jana pulled up in front of the sprawling cedar home in Pacific Beach.

"Sorry. It couldn't be helped. I had a flat."

Twyla wiped her hands on the grimy apron tied around her waist and eyed Jana up and down. "That's what they all say. I thought you were going home to shower and change."

"I didn't have time. I got here as fast as I could. Where's Lucy?"

"Inside setting up the tables and making sure we have enough plates and glasses. I picked her up at her aunt's. Did you get the flowers?"

Twyla peered under the red-and-yellow striped canopy of Jana's truck, and not finding what she was looking for, slapped an open palm against her forehead. "Please don't tell me you forgot."

Jana hadn't, but rather than make herself later than she already was, she'd called and pleaded with the florist to help them out.

"I arranged to have them delivered," she explained while following Twyla indoors.

"Which means we now have a delivery charge."

"But I'm here with two hours to spare," Jana countered. "That must count for something."

Jana had just a moment or so to register that the bottom floor of the house showed signs of a designer at work. Personally it was a little too perfect. Expensive Persian rugs were artfully placed on the blonde bamboo floors, and trendy artwork adorned the walls.

She followed Twyla up a short flight of stairs leading to an open living-and-dining area. On the second floor, windowed walls yielded a breathtaking ocean view and the skylights in the vaulted ceilings brought the outdoors in, providing a light airy feeling. Even so, the house seemed sterile. A lot of it had to do with the white-on-white walls and the furniture that was primarily leather, glass, and chrome.

White walls, white Italian leather furniture, cream and white rugs, glass coffee tables with chrome stands. Blah!

The woman who'd identified herself as Iris Sandifer's assistant had been ultraspecific. It was important that the party planner coordinate the rented tables, chairs, and linens. Even the flowers needed to match the home's décor. And to emphasize her point, she'd gone so far as to email photos of the interior of the house.

Still Jana hadn't expected something this austere. It was all too perfect and reminded her of her parents' home—"The Museum," she called it—with furniture more for show than actual comfort. Neither of her parents could tolerate disorder and consequently Jana hated order. It cramped her style and stifled the creative process. Jana had often wondered how the two had produced a child who lived the life of a Bohemian.

"Well, it's about time you showed," Lucy Santana said

cheekily when she spotted Jana. She looked up from the napkins she was folding into bishop's hats. "The ice sculptures should be arriving any moment, we hope, and the bakery has yet to deliver the cake. I've called them twice but they've blown me off. Maybe you can try."

"What about the jazz guitarist?" Jana asked. "Have we heard from him? The last I knew he'd come down with a cold and was thinking of sending a replacement. I informed him he needed to call us with the name of that person."

"I haven't heard a thing," Lucy said, returning to her bishop's hats. "Just pray he shows up."

Twyla handed Jana an apron. "Might as well get busy. There's shrimp to peel. When you're done call the florist and bakery. And while you're at it better make sure we have some kind of entertainment."

"I will, I will." She looked around and said sotto voce, "Where's the host?" There'd been no sign of another person except them.

Twyla shrugged her shoulders. "Mrs. Sandifer was here when I arrived but I think the coordination of this whole thing was too much for her. She took off."

"A woman owns this mansion?" This from Jana.

"Yup. She's an attorney for the city. She's divorced and on the city council."

"Cool," Lucy added, sounding impressed. "One day I'm going to be just like her. I'll have money to burn."

Not if you continue the way you're going, Jana thought but didn't say. She removed the shrimp from the coolers sitting on the kitchen counter, and began peeling and deveining them.

"The guest of honor is retiring, right?" Jana asked a few minutes later.

"Yes, a judge that Iris Sandifer knows. I think they might be going together."

The next two hours went by in a flurry of activity. First the florist showed up with the wrong arrangements. It took some creativity to turn them into pieces that would be acceptable. There was that awesome challenge of matching the décor. The ice sculptures required more manpower than just the driver to get them inside. Lucy, Twyla, and Jana to the rescue again. But at least the entertainer came through. He was a bit nasal and drifty but he took his appointed position. Thankfully he wasn't required to sing.

Iris Sandifer, the hostess, showed up forty minutes before her dinner party was scheduled to start. She claimed that her hairdresser had been running behind schedule. She was a gaunt woman with a horse face and an annoying voice. She also had mannerisms most would attribute to a male. But at least she seemed grateful to have them there and in charge of the festivities.

After a perfunctory check on how things were proceeding, Iris pronounced everything perfect and got out of the way.

Fifteen minutes before the party started, Twyla and Lucy had already changed into black slacks and white tuxedo shirts, A Fare to Remember's standard gear. Twyla eyed Jana's wild attire while her fingers stroked her chin. "Hmmmm, we need to do something about you. That T-shirt definitely has to go. It's had its day. What do you have in that bag you're carrying, Lucy?"

"A change of clothes. I packed something to sleep in, plus my waitress uniform."

Lucy had a part-time job at the roller rink. Twyla had offered to have the teenager sleep over if the din-

ner party ended too late. Lucy, anxious to escape anything faintly resembling parental authority, probably
had packed a bag that could take her away for weeks.

Twyla handed Lucy her keys. "Go to the car and get
your uniform out."

The teenager seemed puzzled. "Why?"

"Because you're going to lend it to Jana."

Lucy was already off and running before Jana could
protest. But Jana had no choice anyway. She and Lucy
were roughly the same size, but she probably wouldn't
fit into the slacks Lucy was wearing. Jana's legs were far
more athletic, with well-developed muscles that came
from daily jogging. Other than that, they were both of
average height and weight.

Soon Lucy returned, shaking out the wrinkles on
the outfit. It was made up of a short black skirt, white
blouse, and red apron with ruffles. The thing reminded
Jana of a French maid. But she didn't have much
choice, it was either slip into the getup or stick with
the "I AM WOMAN HEAR ME ROAR" T-shirt. And somehow
she did not think that would go over well with Iris Sandifer and her uppercrust friends.

Jana grabbed the uniform from Lucy, ducked into
the bathroom off the kitchen, and quickly changed.
The skirt was way too short, at least shorter than she preferred. It left exposed a good eight inches between
her knee and thigh. But what choice did she really
have? Casual cropped pants were hardly appropriate
attire for a semiformal event.

A banging on the bathroom door reminded Jana
that she'd taken too long changing.

"The first guest is about to arrive," Twyla shouted. "It's
Judge Greene, our guest of honor. You need to come
out."

Jana emerged in time to see a short, portly man, who reminded her of the Keebler elf, swagger through the front door. He was greeted effusively by the much-taller Iris Sandifer and escorted outside to the patio where a bar had been set up. Twyla now presided behind that bar.

Things moved fast after that. More and more guests began arriving and the valets that Twyla and Jana had hired were kept busy. As the room quickly filled up, it soon became clear there were closer to thirty-five guests rather than the twenty-plus they'd been told to expect.

Jana whispered to Lucy, "Take this tray of canapés out, and while you're serving do a quick count."

Jana then peered through the glass as the teenager circulated amongst the guests. She prayed there would be enough of the main course to go around. The hors d'oeuvres wouldn't be a problem; most would take a nibble and save themselves for the main meal and maybe even dessert.

It was important this engagement came off without a hitch. Iris Sandifer was paying one hundred and fifty dollars per plate and whether the erroneous count was her fault or not, it wouldn't go over well running out of servings. If that meant Jana had to boil pasta, so be it.

Lifting the cover on one of the chafing dishes, Jana peered inside. There would be plenty of lamb at least. She and Twyla had taken bets that it would not be one of the more popular entrées, but Iris Sandifer had requested it, and it might even turn out to be their saving grace.

Jana quickly examined her options. Option one was to talk to their hostess and suggest that instead of serving a sit-down dinner the meal could be served buffet-style. That way she, Twyla, and Lucy could control the portions. Yes, that might very well be the solution.

Jana was pulled back to the present when she heard a female voice say, "Sorry we're late. Iris, this is Reese McDonald, my date. Reese is the urban designer Bruce Rothschild hired to create a vision for Lakeview."

That got Jana's attention. What on earth was Reese McDonald doing here, and with Yvonne Munoz, a fixture on the city council? Jana had thought the designer was new to town and didn't know anyone. With displeasure she noted Yvonne's perfectly coiffed hair and immaculate grooming. The councilwoman sported a designer dress that had to have set her back several hundred bucks while Jana looked like yesterday's leftovers.

To top it off, Jana would now be forced to wait on the man and his date, dressed in Lucy's ridiculous waitress outfit. How humiliating.

Somehow she'd have to blend into the woodwork. How she would manage that she didn't know, but the bigger problem now was running out of food.

Lucy came screeching across the tile floors, her voice carrying. "Jana, Twyla needs more ice and highball glasses. She says she needs them like yesterday."

Iris's raised eyebrows acknowledged Lucy's loudness. "Please take these guests out to the patio while I show the mayor the house."

Jana got the message loud and clear. "Of course, Mrs. Sandifer."

Jana thought she'd recognized the tall redheaded man with his wife on his arm, although in person he seemed more human and less formidable. Acknowledging the mayor with a brisk nod, and conscious that she and Lucy were the subjects of curious glances, she issued an order.

"Lucy, please escort these guests out to the patio."

"Jana, I'd prefer it if you did," Reese said, surprising her while Iris and Yvonne actually gaped.

"Do you two know each other?" Iris asked, looking from one to the other.

"We do." This came from Reese.

Dammit, he'd recognized her, and to think she'd hoped to blend into the woodwork. Now hopefully he wouldn't embarrass her.

Jana managed a tight smile and hoped her panic didn't show. "I need to take care of a couple of things here," she said, her voice modulated. "Lucy will be happy to escort you out."

A bewildered Iris stood by trying to assess the situation while Mayor Sapperstein visibly fidgeted. Iris was no fool. She knew when it was time to move on. "Jana, see to it Ms. Munoz and her date get drinks."

"Of course."

That edict issued, Jana was left little choice than to leave her appointed station. She instructed Lucy to get the ice and highball glasses, and led the way out.

"I'm confused," she heard Reese say from behind her. "You handed me a card that said you were a social worker."

"I am," Jana threw over her shoulder.

"Then why the cute little getup?"

Of course he noticed—and who wouldn't, she supposed. As the hired help, she had to answer. "I'm part owner of an event-planning business. We're catering this event. As you very well know, I was running late and had no time to change clothes so I borrowed this outfit."

"It fits you well," Reese added, his eyes sliding over her. "Who would have guessed you moonlight as a caterer?"

Jana wasn't sure how to interpret his words. Thankfully they were already out on the patio and the noise level prohibited further conversation.

Edging her way around pockets of people, Jana approached a bar that was five-people deep while Twyla, efficient as always, was multi-tasking. She had three drinks started while already taking orders for more.

Reese's date didn't seem to have a lot to say. She was sizing up the situation and still seemed a bit dazed.

Twyla caught Jana's eye.

"What will it be?" her friend asked, her raised voice competing with the jazz guitarist and the general chatter around.

Reese, the consummate gentleman, let his date order first. "Absolut and tonic," he added.

"I'll leave you, then. Dinner should be served in half an hour," Jana said, dashing off.

During the next two hours, Twyla, Jana, and Lucy managed to serve the buffet dinner. Through creative means, by serving nouvelle-cuisine portions, they managed to provide seconds to those who asked. The guests for the most part seemed to be having a good time. Those already slightly inebriated continued to fortify themselves with wine through dinner and well into dessert.

Jana, accompanied by Lucy, had begun picking up dirty dishes when a snippet of conversation caught her attention. The mayor said to a man Jana didn't recognize, "Have you heard about the plans for Lakeview Park? The southeast district has needed a facelift for quite some time. The goal is to make it a real showplace."

"Who's the developer?" his companion, with a face that was tanned to the point of looking like leather, probed.

"Do you even have to ask? Bruce Rothschild, of course." The mayor chuckled. "Got to give the man credit, he's the one with the Midas touch."

Jana slowed down in the general area and pretended to stack plates on a tray. Any information she overheard might serve her well. It paid to keep a clear head especially if what she'd suspected had just been confirmed: the gentrification of Lakeview Park all boiled down to money. No one cared that the people of southeast San Diego were about to be displaced. When those with money spoke the poor and downtrodden didn't have a voice.

"The permits have all been approved and groundbreaking's scheduled for two months from today," Mayor Sapperstein continued. "You'll be on the invitation list, Paul. Maybe Iris will give us the name of these caterers. The food has just been exceptional."

The requisite backslapping and mouthed banalities followed. Jana, instead of being elated that the mayor was impressed by their catering, got angrier by the moment, but this wasn't an appropriate place to vent.

"I'll be there," Paul answered. "What exactly are the plans for Lakeview Park?"

"Ask the urban designer. He's here with Councilwoman Munoz. Why don't you go over and introduce yourself?"

The mayor pointed out Reese and the Munoz woman, who appeared quite taken with him. She was hanging on to his every word, just like she was hanging on to his arm. For some inexplicable reason Jana wanted to strangle her.

"Maybe I'll do just that," Paul said, heading in the direction of the champagne-and-dessert table where Reese and Yvonne were standing.

Guests now began clanging their forks against wineglasses. "Speech! Speech! We want to hear from the man we're honoring."

Endless toasts followed. For the next half an hour, Jana and Twyla were kept busy filling and refilling champagne glasses. As tongues loosened, Jana determined that something needed to be done to save Lakeview Park from the vultures.

Someone needed to take a stand. That someone, she determined, would be her.

Chapter 4

Reese continued on his rounds, his mind busily assessing the options. He'd drawn up preliminary plans for Lakeview Park but there were a couple of key areas that he needed to think about where he'd just drawn a blank. So he'd decided to do another site inspection of the forty acres that made up the property.

He tried his best to focus but found that his thoughts kept returning to the bizarre woman with the curly blond hair that bushed out like a halo. Jana Davis was certainly unconventional, yet she was intriguing on many levels. He'd pegged her as a throwback to the seventies, and it had to do with more than the way she dressed. It was the way she thought as well.

She had an intensity about her that was rare, especially in a world where people had grown callous and no longer had a sense of fair play. Some might call it overly righteous. But there was something compelling about a person who had the courage to stand up for her beliefs. It seemed that if Jana felt strongly enough about something, she had no problem speaking up and taking action.

But for now, better to forget about the woman and concentrate on something else, like the job he was being paid to do. Bruce Rothschild was counting on Reese to meet some tough deadlines. Bruce had gone so far as to dangle a huge bonus in front of him if he completed the plans on time and if, by the next deadline the project was well under way.

Bruce had big ideas for Lakeview Park. He was counting on Reese's design to be in line with his vision. The problem was that Bruce's visions were often consistent with the money he could make, and continually changed.

From the very beginning, the project had excited Reese. He'd practically salivated at the thought of putting his personal stamp on a project that most certainly would garner national press. It would be a major coup to clean up one of San Diego's remaining eyesores. But even as good as it sounded, Reese knew there would be some fallout. And with that knowledge came sadness and a sense of responsibility for those people who would be displaced.

He could relate. He'd been raised in an urban area of Baltimore where every inch of public space was valued. Had it not been for public parks like this, where he'd worked off aggression, he might easily have been another statistic. For the majority of those spending time at Lakeview Park, home was a concrete jungle. It was just the way it was. When you had limited means, you became territorial about these properties. They were the only outlets you had.

Still, much of the park was wasted space and he had an obligation to do something about it. Aesthetically it could be improved by designing beautifully landscaped paths and tinkling fountains. Income-producing buildings could be constructed with retail stores on the ground floors and rental apartments above.

And instead of the one lake that gave Lakeview its name, several man-made lakes could enhance the property's value even more. Along those lakes would be walkways, biking paths, villas, and townhomes. And conveniently located would be little coffee shops and avant-garde boutiques. Reese had even found the ideal spot for the botanical gardens where people would feel free to roam.

Now he paused in front of a run-down basketball court. An intense game of ball was under way, shirts against skins. Based on the grunts, expletives, and heavy breathing, both teams were taking the game seriously.

"Come on, set it up, man," the shortest of them yelled.

"Hey, over here, Drew."

The shouts, expletives, and heavy breathing evoked memories of a childhood that had been far from easy. At times playing ball in the park had been his only means of letting off steam. One team would remove their shirts while the others left them on. That was how you played street ball.

A tall, good-looking teenager with a tapered waist dribbled the ball up court, then turned it over to a teammate. After the shot was made, the ball was dribbled down court and into the hands of the opponent.

"Want to take my place, man?" the tall teenager whom Reese had heard referred to as Drew shouted. "I got someplace to be."

And although he was tempted, Reese couldn't. "Would love to but not today," he said. "I need to get to work."

"Whatever."

Shrugging his shoulders, the boy returned to the

game after a time out. Reese tore himself away from watching ball. He continued to stroll by teenagers in Lycra shorts on rollerblades and past bicyclists in training for some sort of marathon. He had two stops in mind: the square that looked like an amphitheater and the community center.

Both the square and property around the building had unlimited potential. Reese needed to think about what he could do with all that space. For so long it had drawn the elderly and those with time to spare, who on sunny days sat outside reading newspapers and playing unending games of checkers. But at night, the relaxed atmosphere changed. Hypodermic needles and discarded condoms reflected an entirely different crowd.

"Hey, aren't you the architect?" The young female voice came at Reese from nowhere.

He came back to the present to see a Latina teenager, in a too-short denim skirt and silver jewelry, bouncing toward him. She looked vaguely familiar.

"Designer, and who wants to know?" he asked, flashing a smile that hopefully softened his words.

The girl was practically in his face now. "You don't remember me, do you?"

On closer inspection, Reese thought he did. The child was wearing, way too much makeup for his taste.

"I'm Lucy. I was working the party for that retired old guy, the one you attended with that councilwoman."

The teenager meant the party for Judge Greene, the one Bruce Rothschild thought was so important to attend. Bruce saw it as the perfect venue to network. Since the developer had had a prior commitment, he'd had Yvonne Munoz, who needed a date, call Reese up. There were supposed to be no strings attached. Now the woman was becoming a pain. And short of being rude, Reese wasn't sure how to let her know he was not interested.

"Of course I remember you, Lucy," Reese said, flashing another smile her way.

Lucy seemed pleased to be recognized. Her fingers outlined the tattoo of a butterfly encircling her belly button. Reese waited for the next comment.

"You're the guy Jana thinks is full of himself," she said. "The one who's going to take the property and ruin it."

Ah, Jana had been talking about him, at least that was something, though the picture she'd painted was certainly not a very flattering one. If he kept Lucy talking maybe he could find out more about the feisty woman the child seemed to admire. The social worker had been coming to mind more and more.

"Is that what Jana really thinks?" Reese probed. "That I'm obnoxious and out to do no good?"

"She didn't exactly put it like that," Lucy admitted. "I think she just doesn't like you." The teenager took a step toward him, invading his space. "But I do. I told her I thought you were hot."

Reese did not like the direction this conversation was heading. He stepped back.

"Uh, Lucy, I'm flattered but I'm an old man. An attractive young lady like you would do far better with one of the boys playing basketball."

Lucy's voice wobbled. She seemed less sure of herself now. "I went with one of those boys. He dumped me."

Reese felt sorry for the girl. He patted her arm awkwardly. "You can't account for taste now, can you?"

"And I'm pregnant." Lucy patted her flat stomach. "And he doesn't want it. He thinks I should get an abortion."

This was way too much information, at least more

information than he needed to know. Reese remembered Jana's occupation. "Have you discussed your situation with Jana?"

Lucy wrinkled her nose. "Of course I have."

"And what did she say?"

"She wants me to think about it carefully. I'm here today to talk to her about Drew. I was hoping she'd be at the center."

Fortune had played right into Reese's hands. He'd just been given the perfect excuse to find out more about Jana Davis.

"I'll walk with you to the center," he offered. "I was heading that way anyway."

Lucy appeared thoroughly delighted. As they walked, she began chattering in earnest, telling him all about the aunt she lived with, and how difficult it was not to have a real home.

"We need to make sure Lakeview Park remains a place for the people," Jana shouted. She was standing on a chair in the center of the room surrounded by the regulars who came to use Lakeview's facilities. "I am counting on your support."

"We hear you, girl! You got it!" Loud applause followed.

Jana waved the clipboard she was holding in the air. She looked down at the forty or fifty people gathered around her. The energy was palpable. They were totally with her.

She'd left work early and headed over to the community center, figuring that midweek would bring out a decent crowd. She had hoped for an adult group: people with family commitments who couldn't afford the time to hang out on weekends, and young men with budding sports careers. She'd also wanted to catch the overeaters, who, having scarfed down what they could on the weekend, felt guilty and needed to work off pounds.

Jana needed to feel these people out and get their reaction. She'd arrived to a packed gymnasium filled with boxers in training, all banging the heck out of punching bags. The lounge area, more often than not used as a soup kitchen, held the elderly, while the unemployed and underemployed sat in clusters discussing the state of their affairs.

"I'll be passing around this petition for you to sign," Jana added. "What it says is you'd like to be included in the decisions concerning Lakeview Park."

"Yeah. We don't want the man to get over," an elderly woman up front yelled.

The man—meaning white people. Jana didn't like the idea that the situation might be getting racially charged.

"Isn't the architect one of us?" a male voice shouted from somewhere in the bowels of the room.

"Sure, but he's the hired hand," someone said. "He works for the developer. Fixing this place up means money to him."

There was another wild outburst of applause.

"It's always about money. Now where's that petition for us to sign?"

"I'll be passing it around in a minute," Jana explained. "It's not that we're looking to stop the developer. What we want is a piece of the park and to save your homes. This community center has been around for years. You rent it for weddings, you barbecue on these grounds. In summer you swim and row on this lake. Where will you go if this place turns into a fancy development? Your children will be forced to turn to the street."

"No way. Bruce will have to pay," someone in the crowd began to chant. Soon others picked it up.

Excited discussions broke out all around her. The show of support and willingness to take a stand made Jana more confident. Questions were now being fired at her from every angle.

"One at a time, please," Jana responded. "I'll try to answer you as best as I can."

"What's going on here?" a loud male voice barked from the vicinity of the front entrance.

Every head swiveled as normally laid-back Ken Gibson strolled in. He looked as if he was about to panic. Ken did not do confrontation well.

"Jana, what's this meeting about? Why are you up front and center?"

"What we want to know is how come this meeting wasn't called by you?" the same old lady who'd said she didn't want "the man to get over" piped in.

"Yeah. How come we had to read about Lakeview Park in the paper? That Rothschild man wants to turn the place into a fancy development and toss our people out." This came from somewhere in the middle.

Ken managed to gently push his way through the milling group and toward the center of the room. Spotting the clipboard that was now being circulated, he turned to Jana. "What's that?"

She was about to explain but was cut off. Questions were being hurled at Ken from every direction. Since he was the community relations director, he was supposed to have answers.

A chant began in the back of the room: "We demand to know what's going on. We demand to know what's going on."

Things were rapidly getting out of control. Jana decided to turn the matter over to Ken. He probably was better equipped to answer the community's questions anyway. She accepted the hands offered and stepped down from the chair.

Ken, looking like he would rather be any place but here, took the spot she vacated. He gave the time-out sign and slowly the room began to quiet.

"I'll attempt to tell you what I know."

"About time," someone shouted.

"Lakeview Park was leased to the city of San Diego."

"Yeah, yeah we already know that."

"Okay, then you probably already know that the owner has now turned it over to a developer."

"Break it down and just tell us what the plans are," one of the boxers screamed.

"Plans. Uh, well I'm not sure. There's been a lot of discussion but I haven't seen the actual designs yet."

"Liar."

Ken, although flustered, rallied. "When I do I will be sure to share that information with you."

"What's going to happen to our center?" the little old lady up front asked.

"What about the facilities, the picnic grounds, and basketball courts? Will we have use of them?"

"I'll attempt to get all those answers for you. Soon. I promise."

"That's not good enough."

Jana actually felt sorry for Ken. She could tell from the restlessness of the crowd they were not satisfied with his answers. Meanwhile her petition was being circulated and people were busy signing it. A good thing, she thought.

The crowd began to chant again. "We want answers. We want answers."

Whatever else Ken planned on saying didn't happen. The crowd started to boo and he just stood there looking helpless.

Reese walked in to a totally chaotic scene. Everyone seemed to be talking at once, yelling, or booing. A few people were chanting in the back of the room, words he couldn't make out. What the hell was going on? The teenager accompanying him looked pretty bewildered too.

"Why is Ken standing on that chair?" Lucy asked.

"Probably an impromptu meeting."

"And what's Jana doing talking with these people?"

He had a sneaking suspicion that he knew what they were up to. "I guess we'll soon find out," he said.

He and Lucy stood at the back of the room assessing the situation and waiting to hear something from Ken.

"What's that thing people are signing?" Lucy asked after a while. She pointed out a heavyset man scribbling on a clipboard, which he quickly handed off to someone else.

Reese watched the paperwork circulate and finally got the picture. The community had grown restless and were circulating a petition. It probably had something to do with stopping the plans for the Lakeview Park development from moving ahead .

Just what he needed. While the park was private property, and technically the people had no say, the lack of local support could make things damn uncomfortable. It could even hold up some important permits.

"I'm going to see what's going on," Lucy said, taking off.

Reese watched her stop to ask a man in a sweat suit

a question. She then made a beeline for Jana, pushing through the crowd surrounding the social worker. The two had a brief exchange and Lucy pointed him out. Before he knew it his nemesis was heading over and, the crowd followed her.

Ken Gibson, who was still standing in the center of the room on a chair, eyed the progress of the people trailing Jana. Spotting Reese he waved.

Shouting above the din to make himself heard, Ken said, "If you want answers, the designer working the project is here. He's standing in the back of the room."

To Reese's great surprise the executive director proceeded to point him out.

What a wimp!

Reese barely had time to take a deep breath before he was surrounded by people.

Chapter 5

"What possessed you to get these people all riled up?" Ken asked Jana when they were back in his office. "You're supposed to remain neutral and not get involved."

Jana, who'd refused the seat he offered, stood facing him, arms crossed. "I'm not an employee of Lakeview Park, I just volunteer. Sometimes you have to take a stand for what you believe."

"Look, Jana," Ken said, "I don't want problems. Bruce Rothschild is a powerful man. He's not going to be happy if these folks get in his way. If I were you I'd try talking to the designer privately. Maybe you could charm him."

Jana hiked an eyebrow. "Charm him into?"

"Seeing things your way. He's designing over forty acres of property. Maybe if you batted your eyelashes just the right way, he could talk the developer into keeping a small portion of the park public. If you get nasty he may just dig his heels in."

Jana stood there for a moment, speechless. Did Ken really think that she would be willing to cozy up to the architect or whatever the man called himself? He was basically asking her to prostitute herself for a piece of land she didn't even own.

"I'm not interested in batting one eyelash in that man's direction," she answered, her voice firm. "Did you hear Reese's little speech? The arrogance of him." Jana lowered her voice several octaves and puffed out her chest. "'We want to make this park safer for you. Gentrification is bound to drive out a certain element.'" Then her voice rose, returning to its normal, lilting cadence. "'Lakeview Park has been stagnant for too long. It's time for a change.'" Now who the hell is he to say that? He didn't grow up here. He's a hired hand flown in from Baltimore."

"You're getting yourself all worked up over nothing," Ken said, trying to placate her. "And you practically started a riot when you asked him what his plans were for affordable housing. Did you hear the old lady call him a Tom?"

Jana chuckled. "Good for her, and she wasn't the only one. Several others mumbled the same thing under their breath. People deserve to have their questions answered and in a manner they understand. He gave them a bunch of hogwash and they called him on it. Who is he to speak down to these people?"

Realizing he wasn't making headway, Ken shook his head. "Oh, Jana, you're one of the most openminded people I know. And you're of mixed heritage so why are you so hard on the guy?"

What did her interracial heritage have to do with anything? She knew what she was. Thankfully, a knock on Ken's door interrupted the lecture in progress.

"I'll be with you in a minute," Ken called.

"Is there anything else you'd like say to me before I take off?" Jana asked, glancing at her watch and realizing that she would be late for dinner with her parents.

"No, I'm just counting on you to keep a cool head. We get enough drama here at the center as it is. Use your influence to keep things calm."

Jana slid the clipboard with the signed petition under one arm and prepared to leave. At the closed door she turned back. "Ken, I can't promise you to sit back and watch Bruce Rothschild and his cronies turn Lakeview into a model neighborhood where only perfect people live. But I'll do my best to ensure there are no ugly confrontations."

"That's all I ask."

Jana didn't wait to be officially dismissed. She threw open the door and almost bumped into Reese.

"Sorry."

He grasped her by the shoulders, steadying her and stopping her at the same time. "Not so fast. You and your buddy just threw me to the wolves." One hand now clutched his chest. "I'm still recovering from the beating I got."

Jana disentangled herself. She refused to acknowledge that his touch had the most unsettling effect.

"You're here to see Ken. Why don't I leave you two to talk?"

"This situation concerns you as well. Aren't you the one who started the petition?"

Ken was still standing there staring at them. He hadn't come to her defense and wasn't about to.

"Something had to be done to protect these people's rights," Jana answered, trying to walk around Reese.

"Why does that someone have to be you? You're trying to sink me, and we don't even know each other."

"And I'd like to keep it that way," Jana said, letting herself out.

Almost an hour and a half later—because she'd stopped by her apartment to change—Jana pulled up in the circular driveway of her parents' sprawling home in upscale La Jolla. Carmen, her parents' part-time housekeeper, let Jana in. At one point Carmen had been both nanny and housekeeper. Now she came in three days a week.

"Hola, chica, Mama and Papa pretty much gave up on you. But I knew you would come through," Carmen said gruffly, after accepting Jana's kiss.

Jana gave the housekeeper a big hug. "Where are they anyway?"

"Seated and eating. You know how rare it is to have them both home at the same time. Your father is on call and that beeper could go off at any moment. Better make the most of your time together."

Jana's father's specialty was obstetrics and gynecology. Her mother was considered one of the best heart surgeons in the business and so she was constantly in demand. Jana decided it was best to join them on the patio and quickly because, as Carmen said, having everyone together at the same time was rare.

Bourbon, the family's golden retriever, came bounding in, almost knocking Jana over. Fur flying and tongue hanging, she began jumping in an attempt to lick Jana's face.

"Easy, girl."

Jana stopped briefly to wrestle with the dog, who drooled excitedly as Jana scratched behind her ear.

"Bourbon," Jana's father called from outside, "get out here now. You're not allowed in the house."

The dog ignored the order, and wagging her tail, walked alongside Jana.

As Jana sailed through the elegant French doors separating the library from the patio, Bourbon kept pace. As Carmen had mentioned, both doctors were seated and halfway through their meal.

"Hi, Mom. Hi, Dad. Sorry I'm late," Jana said.

Mona Davis raised her head, eyeing Jana up and down.

"Late is an understatement." Jana's mother tapped the face of her watch. "You were supposed to be here almost two hours ago. Are you still eating just vegetables? You're as skinny as a rail."

Jana decided to ignore the chiding. She looked down at her black cotton dress with the pink poodle on the skirt. A matching pink belt cinched her waist. She'd thought it looked pretty, and still did, despite furry signs of Bourbon's affection creating tan against black.

"I'm sorry. It couldn't be helped," Jana repeated. "I got stuck at an unexpected meeting."

"Well the important thing is that you made it," her father, who still had a full head of blond hair, added. "We were worried about you. Come here and give us a kiss."

Jana dutifully kissed both her mother and father. Whenever she was in her parents' company she was back to being the messy, disorderly child who'd forgotten to pick up her toys. She often wondered why she constantly felt the need to apologize.

"The setting opposite your mother is for you," Gordon Davis pointed out. "And by the way, I think you look pretty and not too thin at all." He snapped his fingers. "Come here, Bourbon, sit."

Jana sat in her allotted seat. Bourbon, who'd ignored his master's command, found a spot lying on Jana's feet.

Carmen came by to pour water and serve Jana fresh vegetables and pasta. She respected Jana's right to be a vegan. Whenever Jana dropped by for dinner the housekeeper made sure she had something she could eat.

Halfway through the meal, Mona—who'd been busy quizzing Jana about her single state, not having received the answers she wanted—switched the conversation. "How about next week you and I go shopping? We'll need to get you some decent clothes."

"What's wrong with my clothes?" Jana asked, returning to twirling her pasta. She eyed her mother suspiciously. "I've got more in my closet than I can possibly wear."

Mona sniffed loudly. "You're twenty-six years old, honey, and in a profession that must require you wear business suits. All day long you interface with people."

"And so do you," Jana threw back. "Normally you wear a long white coat over a skirt or a pair of slacks."

"That might be so but I'm also not wearing someone else's castoffs perfumed with body odor. Just think how unsanitary that is."

"Okay, okay. Time out, ladies," Gordon said, pressing the tips of his fingers against one palm. He was the peacemaker. "Go shopping. A little female bonding with each other wouldn't hurt. I'll even foot the bill if you call a truce, provided you both buy something nice."

Mona perked up noticeably. "Would that include a St. John's suit by chance?"

"Anything your little heart fancies, dear. Just as long as I don't have to declare bankruptcy when you're done."

"Now that that's settled, let's talk about when," Mona piped up. "What's your schedule look like, Jana?"

Jana searched for a good excuse but nothing came to mind quickly.

"You need clothes," her mother prodded. "That dress has to be one of your 'finds.'"

Jana heaved out a sigh. She was beginning to regret accepting the dinner invitation. Not that her mother's carping was anything new. Growing up in an anal environment made her hate structure.

"Mona!" Gordon warned. "Enough! Jana has her own style. Not everyone has to wear St. John's suits to look wonderful."

Gordon's beeper went off and he groaned. Unclipping the device from his belt, he glanced at the number and stood. "Time to go to work, looks like Mrs. Miller might be delivering earlier than planned."

It had always been like this, one or the other, if not both parents on the run, beautiful meals grabbed hastily and elaborately planned vacations ruined. A house designed for functionality and style rather than for comfort and relaxation. An only child made to feel as if she was in the way.

No wonder Jana had learned independence at an early age. And she'd also deeply resented a mother who never seemed to have time for her. Other children's mothers showed up at school and for dance recitals, but not hers. Yet deep down, Jana knew her parents loved her. They just never quite understood what made her tick. As a result they were unable to get through.

Carmen handed Gordon a paper sack whose contents would be his midnight snack. And Mona checked to make sure her husband had his wallet and cell phone. She sent him off with a kiss. On his way out he stopped to hug Jana.

"Don't be a stranger, baby."

And finally it was Jana and her mother alone, seated at a patio table surrounded by palms. Mona was holding a pocket organizer she'd taken from the jacket pocket of her black pants suit and was busy pushing buttons.

"What day is good?" she asked.

"Mother, I work."

"Work ends at some time and stores close at nine. We can start with Neiman Marcus."

"I can't afford Neiman Marcus."

Mona pursed her full lips. She was a dark-chocolate woman with liquid eyes and a smooth complexion that women half her age envied. Now those huge, unblinking eyes stared at Jana.

In one of the few intimate moments Jana and her father had ever shared, he'd admitted he'd taken one look at the determined woman sitting in the front row of his class at med school and was a goner, different pigmentation be damned.

"Your father has already told you he'd pay," Mona said after a while. "We'll do a little shopping and then I'll treat you to dinner."

"All right, Mother. Wednesday it is, but I'd rather have the money being spent on an outfit go to pay for advertising for my business instead."

Mona signaled to Carmen for decaffeinated coffee. "The business hasn't folded? You can't even cook."

That showed how little Mona knew. When Jana was growing up, while Mona was working at the hospital, Carmen taught Jana to cook and clean house. The housekeeper had even taken Jana home with her so that she could play with her five children. Carmen didn't worry about things like scuff marks on tile floors and whether her sofa was stained. Carmen's house was a home.

Jana now feigned a yawn. "I'm exhausted, Mother. Time to go home. It's been a brutal day."

"There's always your old room. You could stay here."

"Thanks, but I didn't bring clothes."

"That's an excuse."

Jana started for the door. Mona followed her. "See you Wednesday then, darling?"

"Whatever, Mother. Thanks for dinner, Carmen," Jana called.

Then Mona surprised her by saying, "What's going on with Lakeview Park? Every time I pick up the paper there's some article about the developer and the African American designer brought in. I'd think prettying up that place wouldn't be half bad. It's needed a face-lift for quite some time."

"Perhaps, but think about the people being displaced. Where are they supposed to go? I've tried reasoning with the designer but he isn't overly concerned."

Reasoning wasn't exactly what she'd call it but Mona didn't need to know about their bickering.

"You've met the guy?" Mona seemed both surprised and excited. "And what did you think?"

"Unfortunately, there's nothing to think. He's tall, sort of rangy, and melon-colored."

"Good-looking I hear."

"I wouldn't know."

"He must be because he's up for auction at the charity brunch Professional Women of San Diego is throwing. The one I've arranged for A Fare to Remember to cater."

Jana almost swallowed her tongue. "What? Reese McDonald is taking part in a bachelor bid?" The last part finally registered. "Mother, you've gotten us a job?"

Forgetting that Mona didn't particularly like to be hugged, Jana threw her arms around her.

"Yes, baby, the job is yours," Mona repeated and gently disentangled herself. "Kitty Rothschild, Bruce's wife, put your designer on the block for the silent auction. Doubtful he can say no, Bruce is his boss."

Jana laughed until her sides ached. Reese McDonald was getting his just desserts. She would be there to see his humiliation, and she didn't even have to be a fly on the wall.

Chapter 6

Reese found parking a couple of blocks from City Hall. It was the perfect California day and after locking the Range Rover he began walking toward C Street. Around him palm fronds and blooming bougainvillea swayed. In the far distance he could even spy a tiny bit of blue ocean. He was really starting to like San Diego and its laid-back ways.

As Reese approached City Hall, he noticed a large group of blacks and Latinos on the sidewalk. All five percent of San Diego's African American population seemed to be out in full force. As Reese got closer he spotted the picket signs. Damn! Gaining access to City Hall would not be easy and he didn't know the area well enough to know where there was another entrance.

Why did he pick today of all days to apply for permits? Then again would it really have mattered? Most who picketed were committed to a cause. His time today was limited to begin with. In less than an hour he had a working lunch with Bruce Rothschild and he couldn't afford to be late.

He just had to figure out a way around this unexpected hassle. Reese examined his options. He could stride right by the picketers and hope no one recognized him. He could feign interest in whatever their cause was, be empathic, and move on. Or he could walk around them.

Somehow he didn't think of slinking by as an option. It wasn't his style. The lettering on the picket signs was clearer now. Slinking by or feigning interest was definitely not an option.

SAVE LAKEVIEW PARK FOR THE PEOPLE!

REESE GO DESIGN A MCDONALD'S!

BRUCE HAS A RUSE! BRUCE HAS A RUSE!

The message was loud and clear and meant for him. Someone had tipped off these folks that he was coming. He could only hope that time was on his side and no one had spotted him yet.

Too late! The crowd on the sidewalk began to chant.

"Go design a McDonald's! Yeah, go design a McDonald's!"

Reese gave the crowd an *A* for being ingenious. Privately he didn't blame them for taking action. He was doing the job he was paid for. And although he might be sympathetic to those poor and needy, they more than anyone else knew that life wasn't fair.

Determined to brazen it out, Reese decided to ignore the chanting. He would enter the building, take care of business, then be on his way. He tried giving the group a wide berth but they surrounded him.

"We want to know what will become of Lakeview Park." one woman demanded.

"We want affordable housing!" another man cried.

With raised voices they continued to chant. Reese was conscious of time ticking by and of his luncheon engagement across town.

"You'll get updated information," he promised. "The developer will keep you informed."

"When will the meeting be? We want answers."

The chanting began again, this time louder while the picketers circled.

"Soon! Soon! I'd give it no more than two weeks."

Reese began edging his way toward the entrance. The picketers followed, looking as if they would riot at any moment.

An authoritative male voice boomed through a bull-horn. "Break it up, people. Permit or not, you're being disruptive. No hassling."

A couple of police cruisers had pulled up in front. The crowd, spotting the cops, quickly dispersed, and Reese, seizing the opportunity, sprinted into City Hall.

An hour later, he was seated at Mojo's in the tony Gaslamp District. This was another area that had undergone gentrification and now catered to those wanting to see and be seen. It had once been a haven for the homeless and drunks.

Bruce introduced Reese to Seth Bloom, Rothschild's vice president of acquisitions, and quickly got to the business at hand.

"I like most of what you've shown me so far," Bruce said while they waited for their waitress to return with their order. "But there seems to be a lot of unused space that could be revenue-generating. I have visions of income-producing properties: like a martini or wine bar, maybe a day spa for the ladies, and dockage rights on the lake that could be leased."

"I meant to talk to you about that," Reese answered as their waitress set down his plate of mahi-mahi. "I'd hoped to keep that space public. Maybe design a green where the community could stroll. I'd make sure there were several piers where people could fish. The basketball courts could be given a facelift, and tennis and squash courts added. Heck, we could throw in a community pool. Recreational facilities open to the public would send a positive message and bring the dissidents over to our side."

Seth Bloom spoke up. "I think that's a lousy idea. Isn't the whole point to get rid of the element that's taken over Lakeview Park? Heck, most upstanding citizens are petrified to be in that general vicinity after dark."

"I'm reluctant to go there at any time of day," Bruce popped in glumly. "You're right, Seth. Every undesirable this city harbors can be found at Lakeview Park."

Reese found both men's comments offensive. He had a pretty good idea that undesirable might be synonymous with black, since it was mostly people of color who used the Lakeview facility.

"Strange, but I haven't had a problem," Reese spoke up, "other than being verbally attacked by people who feel they're being pushed out. Perhaps if someone on the development end spoke to them like people and quieted their fears, they'd come around. Right now speculation is running rampant."

"I thought you held a meeting," Bruce said, looking at him over the top of his fork before digging into a huge chef salad, liberally sprinkled with chunks of blackened chicken.

"I did because I had no choice. From their perspective I'm the hired gun. I think we should call a meeting that I attend with a PR representative from the organization. That way we can address their concerns."

Seth Bloom made a rude sound with his mouth. "Why bother? It's a waste of time mollifying these people. It's not their property and they're in no position to call the shots."

Reese was really beginning to dislike the man. Somehow he managed a tight smile. "These people, as you put it, can make life quite difficult for all of us. They can hold up permits and bring a lot of negative publicity to the project. We don't need that."

"Let me think on this," Bruce Rothschild said, apparently beginning to see the light and attempting to smooth things over. "On another note, both of you gentlemen have been recruited by my wife, Kitty, to help with a charity event."

Glad the topic had been changed, Reese forced enthusiasm into his voice and said, "Of course we'll help out where we can. What does Kitty need—donations?"

"More like we're kissing pigs or babies," Seth quipped cynically. He had something of a sense of humor, albeit a warped one.

Bruce chuckled and polished off the last of his salad. "You're not far off. You're both up for auction."

"Up for auction?" Reese arched an eyebrow.

He had a sneaking suspicion he knew what that meant but he wanted Bruce to confirm it.

"We're participating in a charity bachelor auction?" Seth confirmed, eyebrows practically touching the ceiling. "Sweet!" He patted his stomach. "Gotta start doing more sit-ups."

The whole thing didn't sound at all sweet to Reese, but what could he say to the man who was his employer? His only choice was to go along with it, or sulk. Sulking usually got you nowhere. Besides, it wasn't as if he was involved with anyone. If San Diego was to be his home for the next couple of years, maybe he needed to start looking for a compatible mate.

Jana completed a challenging counseling session with a young single parent who'd been a walk-in. The woman was visibly distressed and Jana had listened to a long, convoluted story without interrupting. After they'd gotten a few things straight and set up another appointment, Jana was escorting her out when the phone rang. They said a quick good-bye and Jana raced back to answer it.

"Planned Parenthood. This is Jana," she said.

"How are you?"

The deep male voice was one she could not identify immediately.

"Who is this?" she asked, thinking that it might be one of the rare men who came in for counseling. There was always that tendency to be familiar.

"It's Reese McDonald. Are you available for coffee or a drink this evening?"

Jana was so surprised by his invitation she was momentarily rendered speechless. How had he tracked her down at Planned Parenthood? And why was he interested in seeing her socially?

"Jana, are you there?"

"Yes, I'm here." Now curiosity took over. "Where did you have in mind?"

"I was thinking the Marine Room in La Jolla."

"That's awfully fancy."

Since he was going all out, he must want something badly.

"It's a totally different atmosphere during the week

I'm told. Much more informal. We can sit at the bar, have our drinks, and watch the sun go down. I can swing by and pick you up if you'd like."

It was the last thing she needed, being cooped up in the same vehicle as Reese McDonald, a man she didn't particularly like.

If she had her own car and she didn't like what he had to say she could be on her way.

"That's really kind of you but how about I meet you there?" Jana countered.

A pause followed. "What time's good for you?"

Jana glanced at her watch. Her last appointment of the day was due to arrive in ten minutes.

"How does six thirty sound?" That would give her time to freshen up and take a leisurely ride to the restaurant, one of San Diego's landmarks and not exactly in her budget.

"Okay. I'll be waiting out front." Reese then rattled off his phone number while Jana hurriedly scribbled it down.

The rest of the day went by quickly and soon Jana was on Interstate 5 and heading toward La Jolla. She'd cranked the radio up full volume and was singing along to an old Supremes' tune. Oftentimes she thought of herself as being born thirty years too late.

Her thoughts were now on Reese and the upcoming meeting. It was probably more appropriate for him to meet with Ken Gibson. Nothing personal, but she and Reese McDonald were two very different people.

Jana was so deep in thought she almost missed the La Jolla Village Drive exit. After heading west, she got to the third signal and made another left before proceeding downhill another two miles. The whole effect was as if she was driving into the ocean: exhilarating and scary at the same time. Finally she was at Spindrift where the restaurant was located.

Jana handed her truck over to a valet and walked with purpose to the front door. There was no sign of Reese waiting. The smell of ocean followed her every step of the way, a scent she had always loved. It reminded her of weekend trips to the beach. Bracing for the inevitable, she prepared to enter the Marine Room, a place her parents frequented. She'd been here a time or two, but never on a date.

This is no date. More like a business meeting.

Jana walked into the unpretentious-looking building with the beachlike atmosphere. She'd always loved the floor-to-ceiling windows, especially during high tide when waves splashed against the panes.

Since she'd arrived before Reese, might as well use that to her advantage. She took a seat at a bar that was far from crowded, and crossed one athletic leg over the other. The miniskirt she was wearing hiked up and she adjusted the hem. Jana fiddled with her white shirt and its leg-of-mutton sleeves, making sure it was tucked in at the waist. She stared down at her feet in platform sandals that were the same blood red as her skirt.

Where the hell was Reese McDonald?

A bit irked that he was late, Jana twisted a hoop earring and prepared to wait. To occupy her time, she stared out at the ocean while casting occasional glances at the entrance.

"What are you drinking?" the female bartender asked, after Jana had been sitting there a while. A hand with the wrist wreathed in a tattoo added ice to a glass.

"I'm meeting someone. Do you have bottled water?"

Best to keep a clear head, at least until she heard Reese out.

"One water with a twist of lime coming up," the bartender confirmed, moving away.

Jana sensed Reese's arrival before she actually saw him. Maybe it was because a lot of eyes were now focused on the front entrance or maybe because she heard the bartender's quick intake of breath. Whatever, Jana knew he'd arrived.

She turned her stool around in time to witness Reese's majestic entrance. He swept in full of self-confidence, looking like he might have come off a yacht. His khakis had knife-sharp creases and his blue pinstriped cotton shirt, worn under a navy jacket, remained open at the neck. He definitely had that upwardly mobile look. Even his highly polished loafers were a well-known designer's. From the top of his closely cropped hair to his well-shorn feet this was a man who took care of himself.

"Check out what just walked in," the bartender muttered to a female seated on the opposite side of the bar. "Boy would I like to bite into a piece of him."

Jana couldn't hear the woman's response but did note the body language. Her companion at the bar was now sitting up straight, twirling her hair, hoping Reese would notice her.

Reese stood for a moment, scanning the vicinity and looking for Jana. Deciding it was time to make her presence known, Jana stood and waved a hand at him. He acknowledged her with a nod and hurried over.

Jana couldn't help overhearing what the bartender grumbled under her breath. "Shoot! He can do better than that."

She supposed she should be insulted but coming

from a tattooed babe, that really didn't say much. She glared at the woman and turned back to Reese.

"Sorry I'm late," he said extending his hand. "You look great."

Jana shook the hand he offered but couldn't bring herself to say the same. It wasn't because Reese was unattractive, far from that. Realizing all of a sudden her mouth had turned to cotton, she sipped her water and set down the bottle. "You're not late. I was early."

Reese slid onto the stool beside her. "Well at least I'm in time to see another memorable sunset. Take a look at that sky." He then looked out the windows, commenting, "Where do all these sandpipers and pelicans come from?"

He sounded awed by the beauty surrounding him. This was a side she had not seen before. Jana gazed around her, drinking in the fading sunlight dappling the water and a sky that had turned beautiful shades of pinks, blues, and purples.

"What are you drinking?" Reese asked before he spotted her water. "Maybe I can tempt you with something stronger."

She was about to protest, then changed her mind. One alcoholic drink wouldn't kill her. She'd order something festive and flirty.

"Okay, a margarita, please," she said.

"Great. I'll join you."

Jana had never thought of a margarita as being a particularly manly drink but Reese's choice did indicate his self-confidence. And that was a trait she deeply admired.

He placed their orders, swiveled his bar stool, and looked around. "This is quite the place."

"Yes, it is."

"And you're probably wondering why I asked you to meet me here."

"Yes, I am."

The female bartender set down their drinks and then went off to talk to the woman across the bar.

Reese picked up his glass and clinked it against Jana's. "Cheers! I wanted to discuss the Lakeview Park development and run some thoughts by you."

"You need my approval?"

"Not necessarily your approval, just your take on things. You know the community better than I do and you seem to be sensitive to what people need."

She was surprised that he'd given any thought to the people. Maybe she was wrong about him. Perhaps behind that polished exterior was a man who really cared.

"I'd like to keep some space public for the general enjoyment of the people using the park," he said.

"What about the community center?" Jana countered. "What are your plans for that?"

"The building is an eyesore."

"But it does serve a certain social function. It's the only place some of these folks have to meet. The elderly count on coming there to get a warm meal and that might be their only meal of the day."

"What if the center were replaced by a nice public garden and a couple of fishing piers? What if I designed a green or two where people could stroll?"

"That doesn't answer the question of getting people fed," Jana said dryly. She reached over and touched his arm. "Maybe you should talk to the folks and tell them what you're proposing. It would be important to them to feel they were heard."

"I thought about that but this time, rather than

something impromptu, I'm thinking of taking a different approach. Having someone from the Rothschild organization with me might help."

Warming to him, Jana touched his arm again. She was grateful and pleased that he seemed to be coming around.

"That would mean the world to the community and it would send the message that you have heart."

He smiled at her, displaying teeth that weren't exactly even but added to his charm. "Perhaps I should show you just how much heart I have over dinner."

"You're inviting me to dinner after what I put you through?" she exclaimed.

"Why not? I can't think of a more fascinating dinner companion. You're intelligent, principled, and very much alive. You stand up for what you believe in. Those are rare and attractive qualities in today's world."

Jana debated for a moment, then returned his smile. "Okay, I'll join you."

"You will?" Reese seemed pleased by her answer. He signaled to the bartender. "The lady and I are having dinner. Can you find out how long it'll take to be seated?"

Jana wondered what he would be like when business wasn't the main topic.

She would soon find out when she was seated across the dinner table from him.

The one thing she did know is you could get lost in his eyes.

Chapter 7

"Mother, these prices are ridiculous," Jana said, scrutinizing the tag on the elegant suit Mona had picked out for her. She handed the outfit back. "I don't wear Dana. My taste tends to run more to Betsey."

Mona actually seemed hurt that her choice hadn't been received enthusiastically. Jana felt bad. It was rare that she and her mother spent this much time together. One or the other always had something to do. Sometimes she thought maybe that was on purpose.

"You think it's old-fashioned, don't you? We'll just have to find you something more to your taste."

Since when was Mona being so nice and so accommodating?

"It's not just that. These outfits are ridiculously expensive. Combined, they cost more than my rent."

Jana reluctantly followed her mother as she traipsed through Neiman Marcus as if she owned it. And she practically did. Mona willingly paid a fortune for good service.

Her mother's good spirits returned when she spotted a melon-colored silk top. "It's not often we go on a shopping spree funded by your father," she said. "Just pick things you'd enjoy wearing and forget about the cost."

Easier said than done. To pay what the store was asking went against every principle Jana had—not when she could purchase an armload of clothes in one of her consignment stores for the price of just one outfit here. But Mona would not be satisfied unless she bought something. And at least it would help to keep the peace.

She needed something to wear to the brunch A Fare to Remember would be catering anyway. Despite being brunch it was a pretty fancy occasion. A peek in the dress department couldn't hurt.

"Let's take the escalator to the next floor," Jana suggested.

Mona's eyebrows rose but she wisely said nothing. She followed Jana up the escalator and onto a floor that held an assortment of cocktail dresses and couture outfits.

Immediately a sales associate began following at their heels.

"Can I assist you ladies in any way?" she asked.

"We're just browsing."

Mona's polite smile surfaced, though her expression said, "Leave us alone."

Finally the saleswoman left them and Mona wandered away, announcing that she'd seen racks that looked "promising."

The more Jana scrutinized price tags, the more she cringed. Who in their right mind would pay thousands of dollars for clothing they might never wear again? What she needed was something both eye-catching

and sensible, an outfit that would serve several pur-
poses, versatile enough to be dressed up or down.

A discreet sign which read MARKED DOWN, caught her
eye and she made a beeline for those racks. But
marked down or not, the prices were still exorbitant
and almost made her choke.

It took some doing but she eventually found something in line with her style. An ankle-length black skirt
with rhinestones embroidered in tulle spoke to her.
The one drawback was a hole in the hem where someone had caught their heel.

But it was too good a find to put down. Perhaps with
a little negotiation she could get the price down. A little sweet persuading might make the sales help come
around.

The rack adjacent, also MARKED DOWN, yielded a turquoise bustier for a decent price. It came complete
with a matching chiffon scarf à la Isadora Duncan and
would complement the skirt perfectly.

Mona, who had ESP, zoomed over carrying an elegant pantsuit and a cocktail dress draped over one
arm.

"Let's see what you have," she demanded. She tilted
her head to the side, examining Jana's choices and
pronouncing them "out there" but appropriate.

"Get an additional reduction to cover the repair,"
she said, pointing out the hole in the tulle skirt.

"I'm one step ahead of you, Mother."

"With what we save you can get another outfit," she
said, steering Jana toward a rack with pretty sun-
dresses. "How was dinner with that man?"

That man meant Reese. Jana kicked herself for having even mentioned it. She'd gotten home late that
night, and found her mother's message on the answer-

ing machine. And when Jana had called her mother back the next day, she'd let the news slip about the dinner with Reese.

Mona had been excited. An urban designer son-in-law would be a wish come true. She'd been resigned to Jana taking up with an artist or a poet, a man with a headful of dreams and few assets to back up his fantasies. "I'm waiting," Mona prompted.

"A good time was had by all."

"Just a good time?" Mona's eyebrows rose a quarter of an inch.

"What more do you want, Mother? I said I enjoyed myself."

Another sales associate hovered. The initial one had given up and was now stalking a more receptive prospect. Jana pointed out the hole in the skirt's hem. "This is going to cost me a bundle to repair. Is there anything you can do?"

Why even bother mentioning she planned on fixing the problem herself? Jana was actually quite adept with a needle and thread. This skill she'd also learned from Carmen.

"I'll talk to my manager and see," the associate said, taking the skirt from her and disappearing.

But Mona wasn't done. She continued her inquisition while pretending to inspect couture dresses. "So would you say this Reese person is someone you're interested in?"

Jana pretended not to hear.

"Well?"

"He's not my type, Mother. Nor I his."

"Then why are you blushing?"

Couldn't Mona just drop it?

Heightened color was one of the downfalls of being

a light-skinned woman. Jana thought it a perfect time to try on any, if not several, of the dresses her mother had draped over her arm. She raced for the fitting room.

Inside, she replayed the evening spent with Reese. She'd actually enjoyed their time together. During dinner, conversation had covered a myriad of topics. They'd talked about sports and the merits of urbanism. For the most part they'd left alone the tired subject of Lakeview Park. Reese had asked a million questions about her day job and what she found most rewarding about volunteering.

Jana had found him charming, articulate, and attentive. His good manners had even extended to the waitress. A sure sign of what a person's true personality was like, she'd been told. The manner in which a man treated a waitress was the way he'd treat you in a matter of months.

At the end of the evening, Reese had waited with her while the valet brought her truck around. He'd held onto her hand for a moment longer than necessary and thanked her for joining him, sounding like he meant it. But since then she hadn't heard a word from him.

That might be a good thing. Between her day job, volunteering at Lakeview Park, and her event-planning business, she didn't have the time for distractions. Reese McDonald could be a huge distraction.

She would put him out of her mind and concentrate on shopping. Jana slid a lightweight sundress over her head, and glanced at the full-length mirror. The pretty pink frock made her look like a Barbie wannabe. She ditched it.

The next dress, a strapless polka-dot number with a

peplum at the waist, and a fifties' look to it, was more her style. But when she peeked at the price tag, she damn near choked. Buying it was completely out of the question, and not worth a thought.

"Jana," Mona called, growing impatient. "You'll need to hurry. My beeper just went off."

She emerged to find Mona already at the cash register, with charge plate in hand.

"That's pretty." Her mother fingered the material of the sundress and flipped over the price tag. "Not bad as these things go."

"It's outrageous."

"We'll take the dress my daughter is holding," Mona instructed the clerk, "plus the suit and dress I selected, and the skirt with the hole at that good price you offered. Toss the bustier in as well."

"Mother!"

"Hush," Mona said, handing over her charge card. "How often does your father get to spoil you?"

That money could be put to better use. She could use it to promote A Fare to Remember. And it would be money she didn't have to pay back, unlike the loan they'd given her to help fund the business.

The items were quickly bagged and they left.

"Thank you, Mother," Jana said dutifully. "Be sure to thank Dad for me as well."

"Always our pleasure, darling." Mona thrust a couple of folded bills into her palm and blew her an air kiss. "Take your girlfriend Twyla out to dinner. I have to run, baby."

Hopping into her Jaguar she took off.

Dinner with Twyla might not be a bad idea after all. They needed to work out what they were doing about the auction and brunch. They'd not been given much direction except that they'd need to work with the staff at the "Del" where the event was being held.

Jana dug through her cavernous purse and found her cell. The instrument rang in her hand.

A female, clearly sounding distressed, sobbed out her name.

"Ja—na."

It was hard to hear the person. Intermittent yelps on the other end clued Jana in to the gender of the caller.

"Ja—na!" *Sniff!* "Ja—na, it's…"

"Who is this?" Jana interrupted. "What's wrong?"

More sobbing followed and then a pause.

"Take a deep breath," Jana said more gently. "Nothing is that bad. I'll wait until you calm down."

"It's, it's…Lucy."

Jana instantly went on alert. "What's wrong, Lucy?"

"I'm scared. Something's happened," Lucy sobbed.

"Why scared? And what's happened?"

"I'm bleeding, Jana, badly. My stomach hurts."

The teenager began to cry again. Amidst her sobs she told a disjointed story. Jana managed to get the picture. Something was seriously wrong. Lucy needed the emergency room.

"Get into a taxi," Jana ordered. "I'll pay the fare. I'll meet you at Mercy Hospital."

Having dinner with Twyla was now out of the question. Lucy most likely was having a miscarriage. Poor, unfortunate child. The teenager's life was difficult enough, now this, although some might say it was a blessing. Jana doubted the aunt Lucy lived with would be supportive. She probably didn't know the teenager was pregnant. And when she found out there would be hell to pay.

Jana sprinted to her truck and burnt rubber getting out of the parking lot. She made it to Mercy Hospital in less than fifteen minutes. Lucy was not waiting in a taxi out front and Jana grew anxious. She raced into the emergency room, looking around.

"Has a Lucy Santana signed in?" she huffed as she approached an attendant who appeared to be keeping track of people's comings and goings. "Can you check your sheets?"

The man barely looked up at her. He grunted, "Who are you—friend or relative?"

"Both friend and relative."

It wasn't actually a lie. She was probably more family than Lucy had ever had.

"Okay, let's see here." He stabbed a gnarled finger at his sign-in sheet. "There's James, Williams, Montenegro, Phillips, Hoffman. No Santana. Sure she came here? Uh, yeah, wait a minute. She's the girl who was hemorrhaging. The taxi driver was mad as all hell since she bled all over his backseat and no one was there to pay him."

"Lucy is here. Where is she?"

"She was rushed to intensive care."

"I need to be with her. I'm the only thing that child has."

There was a line building behind her of irritated people. She could hear their impatient sighs.

"Please," Jana pleaded. "If you need someone to vouch for me, my friend Twyla Lewis is a hospital employee. She's a social worker."

The stony-faced man, in charge of everyone's fate, fixed her with a stony look, then caved. "I'll see what I can do," he said, moving off. "Wait here." To the people behind her he said, "Sign in. I'll be right back." He poked a finger at the bolted-down clipboard on the podium.

Jana had no choice but to remain where she was and hope that he wouldn't be long. Meanwhile she was acutely conscious of the misery around her and of the unpleasant scents circulating in the air: unwashed bodies mingling with blood. Patients were huddled in various forms of distress, some showing severe pain, others silently suffering.

Five minutes turned to ten, ten to an eternity. The grumblings behind her became more pronounced. Noises were now being made about suing the hospital if someone died or collapsed. At long last the attendant came hurrying back bringing with him a plump Latina nurse.

"That's the woman asking about the girl," he said by way of introduction before quickly returning to his station to deal with the group unrest and riotous spirit.

"Are you Lucy's aunt?" the nurse said, smiling brightly. "I'm Nurse Rodriguez. You're the one she keeps saying is going to kill her if she finds out."

"Actually I'm Lucy's social worker," Jana corrected. Reaching into her purse she found her business card and handed it over. "How is Lucy? Is her baby all right?"

Nurse Rodriguez glanced at the card and then back at Jana. "The baby didn't make it. Lucy is very lucky to be alive. I'm going to pretend you're a relative. Please follow me."

Jana followed the nurse through double glass doors and down a long hallway with gray industrial carpeting. The pea green walls around her added to her growing feelings of depression. She was sick to her stomach and the smell of antiseptic in the air did nothing to help. She grew even more depressed as she passed gurneys filled with people lining the hallway, a sure sign of an overcrowded hospital. No wonder the staff was harried.

Jana heard moans the moment she entered the huge room with drawn curtains. Tired-looking drapes around each bed gave a false sense of privacy. A few haggard doctors with glum expressions were accompanied by equally wan nurses. They made the rounds, going from patient to patient.

"Rodriguez, it's about time you got back," a female doctor snapped. "You're needed." She gestured to a set of closed curtains.

"Lucy's behind the last set," the nurse whispered, pointing down one row and then hurrying off.

Jana dashed in the direction the nurse had pointed. She stopped in front of the closed curtains, paused, and took a breath. *Remain positive, Jana. Put on your happy face. Lucy needs someone upbeat and levelheaded, not worried and out of her mind.*

Bracing herself for whatever she would encounter, Jana called softly, "Lucy, it's Jana. I'm coming in."

She entered and bit back a gasp at the still, pale figure lying on the gurney who appeared tethered to a million lifelines. Approaching she placed a steadying hand on the still form.

"Lucy, honey. How are you feeling?"

"Wishing I was dead."

The voice sounded nothing like the precocious teenager Jana knew. What happened to Lucy was awful and Jana sympathized, but maybe this was the wakeup call the teenager needed, painful as it was.

Lucy had been spinning way out of control for a long, long time. Maybe a higher power had intervened.

Chapter 8

Why was he even thinking about Jana Davis? His mind should be on work and not the troublesome woman who'd set out to ruin him. But even as Reese circled the parking lot of the Lakeview Community Center, his mind remained on the social worker.

Every space was taken and vehicles spilled onto the grass. After a while Reese gave up looking and parked the Range Rover under a tree, and then he sprinted toward the building.

The rickety facility with its peeling surface should really be condemned. It served a useful purpose now but Reese doubted the structure was safe. He'd been mentally preparing for today's meeting and fielding the questions he would answer. Still, visions of Jana Davis kept popping into his mind and he found himself distracted.

He hadn't seen or heard from the woman since their dinner at the Marine Room. But he still thought of their time together. Jana had been good company and her quirky sense of humor matched his. Reese had liked that she didn't play it cool. She was passionate about her beliefs. Her fashion style wouldn't win her any awards but she wore her clothes with a flair that few could pull off.

It had been a while since a woman had captured and held his interest. Call him jaded, but men and women were just not meant to be involved in long-term relationships. He'd learned that firsthand, his own family being the perfect example.

His dad had had four marriages behind him before having Reese and his brother Barry. His parents' marriage probably should never have happened.

Reese's mother had stuck around long enough to give birth to both of them before taking off with the next-door neighbor. She'd never been heard from again.

Left behind was a husband on the late side of fifty totally overwhelmed at the prospect of raising two sons. Maynard McDonald, even at the time of his death, still hadn't completely recovered from his loss. He'd carried with him a permanent look of bewilderment and grief.

Reese had grown up without the usual female role model present. As a result, Reese and Barry had practically raised themselves. Barry had gone on to emulate his father, marrying a succession of women. At not quite forty he was already on marriage number four.

And so Reese had concluded that men and women didn't seem to do well living together. He'd gone the cohabitation route once, but rather than bonding he'd felt trapped. When you grew up in a world with little structure, you valued control.

As a child, Reese had spent hours developing plans in his head. He'd set attainable goals for himself and struggled to make order out of disorder. And so urban design was the perfect career.

Raised voices coming from inside the center told him he'd arrived. Bracing himself for God knew what, he entered. Rhonda Watson, the Rothschild's PR representative should already be there.

The packed room appeared full of despair and turmoil. Reese stood in the back taking the crowd's temperature and trying to assess what was going on.

"This meeting was supposed to start ten minutes ago," he heard someone grumble. "Where's the architect or whatever he's called?"

"Bruce Rothschild needs to get his tired ass down here," someone else shouted.

A chant began. "Bruce! Bruce! Bruce! We want Bruce!"

Whistles, hoots, and hollers followed. Finally a well-put-together African American woman, who looked a little like Secretary of State Condoleezza Rice, peeled herself off a seat and mounted the makeshift dais. She held her hands up for silence. Without a microphone she could barely be heard.

"I'm Rhonda Watson . . ." she shouted over the din.

"Is that supposed to mean something?" one of the agitators shouted back.

"I'm vice president of public relations for the Rothschild Foundation."

"Big deal. You're another Tom."

"Tom! Tom! No, Tomasita!" someone else howled. "We want Bruce. Where's Bruce? Why isn't he here?"

"I represent Mr. Rothschild. He trusts me implicitly," Rhonda bravely shouted.

"Bull. Y'all hear that? She calls him mister," someone yelled from the back of the room.

Reese hadn't expected Bruce's PR person to be African American. But he had to give the developer credit

for being shrewd. It was clever strategy having someone with her pigmentation in a prominent position.
The developer wanted to send the message that his was
a progressive organization. He had two people of color
in important roles.

A barrage of questions was being flung at Rhonda
Watson. She deflected them expertly and shaded her
eyes, scanning the crowd. "Reese, are you out there?"

He had no choice but to step forward.

"Yes, I'm here."

Immediately the crowd began tossing questions at
him and tugging on his arm. With some difficulty
Reese pushed his way to the front of the room.

Ken Gibson appeared in the midst of the melee. He
mounted the dais and clipped a microphone on the
lapel of Rhonda's suit before handing one to Reese.

Rhonda splayed her arms and appealed to the crowd.

"Settle down and we'll attempt to address all of your
concerns. Our vision is to put Lakeview Park back on
the map. If you need specifics, direct your questions to
the man responsible for designing the plan."

Rhonda nudged Reese forward and he joined her.
His gaze scanned the room and he felt an electrical
shock when his eyes connected with Jana's. He was
flustered but quickly rebounded.

She was seated amongst a younger crowd, teenagers
she probably counseled, wearing a fuchsia minidress
with geometric patterns and black fishnet stockings.
The patent leather flats on her feet made her look like
one of the teenagers surrounding her. He acknowledged her existence with a nod.

Jana flashed him the sweetest of smiles. Now he felt
he could take on the world. She'd given him a much-
needed boost of self-confidence. He must have risen a

notch in her estimation because he was doing exactly what she'd suggested: speaking with the people whose lives would be affected.

On the dais, Rhonda rambled on about making Lakeview Park an American dream. She waxed on about it becoming a gated community with picturesque houses. And she talked about the construction of elegant restaurants and bistros, meaning excellent service and no wait in line. When she ran out of embellishments, she referred to the gentrification of Lakeview Park as a return to "*Leave It to Beaver* days," a time when neighborhoods were warm and friendly and people looked out for each other.

"Who's looking out for us?" a woman yelled, tiring of the rhetoric. "We can't afford one of those houses."

"And we don't dine out. We can't afford it," someone else called. "We barely have two nickels to put food on the table. We don't go to la-de-da places where we're not wanted."

It was time to intervene before things got even further out of hand. Rhonda Watson was definitely not reaching these people.

"Why don't I walk you through the plans and then you can ask me questions," Reese interrupted.

"Yeah, bro. You do that."

Reese's speech played up the public areas. He spoke from the heart, sharing his vision for Lakeview Park. He hoped it was in sync with Bruce's but he would find out later. He talked about community pools and piers from which people would fish. Reese then went on to paint a picture of a beautiful green that would be a common area. And he mentioned botanical gardens that would be open to the public.

"Why don't we take questions now?" Reese suggested when he was done. Catching Jana's eye again, he thought she might be perfect to start off with and could actually help to settle down the crowd.

"Jana," Reese called out, "maybe you can speak on behalf of the younger community. What do you see as the primary concern?"

Jana seemed a bit dazed that she'd been singled out but quickly rallied. Getting to her feet she asked, "Why don't you tell us what you have planned for this building? It's currently being used as a community center. What will stand in its stead?"

Trust her to be that direct. He knew instinctively she would not like his answer.

"Suppose you tell me what the community would like to have happen?" he countered.

Answer a question with a question. That's what you did when a subject was controversial and had the potential of blowing up in your face.

"Most of us would like to know that the community center will remain intact," Jana shot back. "The building needs a facelift but it does serve a useful purpose." She looked to the crowd for support. "Isn't that right, people?"

Wild applause broke out around her.

"You said it, girl!"

The status of the community center was a sensitive issue and one requiring a diplomatic response. Personally Reese felt the facility should have been demolished a long time ago. But if he put voice to that they'd eat him alive.

Still, he owed it to them to be straightforward. "The building needs work…"

That produced a huge uproar. It took minutes before the crowd settled down.

"The alternatives are olympic-sized community pools, the botanical gardens, and those attractive fishing piers."

"How's that supposed to help us?" a man, whom Reese guessed was a boxer, shouted. "Where we suppose to work out?"

"There's always the Y," Rhonda countered, making things worse.

Her comment was soundly booed. The core of an apple barely missed her head. Things were fast whirring out of control.

"Okay, okay! Settle down," Ken Gibson shouted, looking like he was close to having a stroke.

The crowd acted as if he hadn't spoken. A chant came from the middle of the room. "Save our community center! Save our community center!"

"What about the basketball courts?" a young male voice shouted, when the group ran out of breath.

To get their attention, Reese held up his hands copstyle. Louder grumbling followed, then finally silence. Jana's expression was priceless. Why did he have the feeling he had let her down?

Maybe it was time to get things back on track.

"Look," Reese said, "all we're trying to do is make the park and the surrounding community safe. For far too long Lakeview Park has been a haven for drug addicts and vagrants. The situation gets worse after dark. The property needs a facelift and that's what we're hoping to do."

"Which means we get pushed out," someone else said. "We can't afford expensive houses and fancy boutiques."

"My plans call for affordable housing," Reese reassured. That much was true. He planned on nudging

Bruce along until he came around to his way of thinking.

Then Jana mounted the dais. Smiling affably she stepped in front of Rhonda. The public relations representative was forced to step back.

"And the residents of these affordable homes will no doubt have the use of exclusive health clubs." She was fanning the flames of an already-smoldering fire. "How much will nonresidents have to pay?"

"Most health clubs will allow nonresidents to join," Reese answered, keeping his voice even.

"For a price," someone shouted. "Money we don't have."

Voices were now raised, followed by more grumblings.

Rhonda's expression said she wanted out. Her left eye had begun to tick and her voice wobbled slightly. "Are there other questions?" she asked. "If not we'll need to wrap up this meeting."

"I have a question," one of the grandmotherly types said. "How much longer before we get tossed out on the street?"

"Tossed out? No one is tossing you out."

"Then what do you call it? The minute you break ground we're gone. You won't want to risk the liability of anyone tripping and falling."

It was Jana who, after looking directly at Reese, said, "You owe these people something. Provide them with an alternative recreational facility. Toss them a bone."

The place went silent as they waited for Reese's comeback. Someone even started clapping.

"Amen."

"Amen."

People were on their feet chanting, "Amen! Amen! Amen!"

And although Reese admired her gumption, he felt like strangling Jana Davis for what she had just started.

Chapter 9

"Look at the number of women here for this thing," Twyla commented, elbowing Jana in the waist. "Isn't that Councilwoman Munoz at table number three? I wonder why she came?"

"Wonder no more. I'm sure she's here for Reese," Jana said sourly, looking over in the direction Twyla was staring. "You saw the way she was all over him at that party."

Yvonne Munoz was at a table with several women wearing ridiculous hats, some of which looked like they might be good launching pads for rockets.

"And you sound jealous, missy."

"I am not."

Twyla should know her better than that. They'd discussed ad nauseum Jana's decision to give up dating until the business was on more solid footing.

Twyla hiked an eyebrow but said nothing. She kept her eyes on the hotel's wait staff. So far they were doing nicely.

The venue for the brunch and bachelor auction was

perfect, the setting being the ballroom of the famous Hotel Del Coronado. Twyla and Jana were stationed off to the side, making sure they had a good view of the entire event.

It had taken some negotiation before Professional Women of San Diego had reached a compromise with the hotel's management: They'd let the organization bring Twyla and Jana in as event planners. But the meal was to be provisioned, cooked, and served by the Del Coronado's employees.

Up to now everything had gone off without a hitch. Twyla and Jana had nixed the usual cardboard chicken and lumpy scrambled eggs. Instead they'd opted for salmon with wild rice and asparagus tips, beef tenderloin in a wine sauce, and, for those wanting breakfast: fluffy omelettes, quiche, and sausages. The smells now were mouthwateringly good.

As for the décor, they'd wanted something soft and feminine, something that said romance was in the air. They'd chosen coral and mint and the tables were draped in coral-and-mint lace. The tables now overflowed with women of every age.

The centerpieces, a combination of lit candles and cabbage roses, complemented the mint-and-coral china. Altogether it made for an elegant setting. At one hundred and fifty dollars a pop, those attending the Professional Women of San Diego event were getting their money's worth.

"Mmmmm. mmmmm, mmmmm. Girl, you are turned out," Twyla said, fingering the tulle on Jana's black skirt. "Where did you get the threads?"

"Neiman Marcus. You're not looking half bad yourself."

"Thanks. But mine aren't some expensive designer's." Twyla fingered the rhinestones on the cuffs of her champagne silk jacket, then touched the bling in her ears. "This getup is something I found in the back of my closet. How's Lucy these days?"

"Recovering. It hasn't been easy. I think she might be depressed. Jana tugged on her camisole top, making sure her breasts didn't spill. She was still feeling guilty for not wearing her usual bargains. "These pieces were on clearance and my dad sprung for the lot," she explained.

"Nice, dad. Does he want another daughter?" Twyla tapped the face of her watch. "The wait staff needs to move it. Dessert should have been served by now."

On cue, as if someone had overheard her, dessert was wheeled out on a cart decorated with trailing pink and white orchids. Coffee and tea followed in silver pots.

"What do you think?" Jana asked, looking out onto the ballroom filled with people.

"I think we've done a helluva job," Twyla said, laughing. "And we've actually made some money to boot. Your mother looks happy, which in turn makes me happy. And in half an hour I get to check out some hotties. What more could a girl want?"

Jana glanced over at the table where her mother sat amongst female colleagues. It was the table close to the Munoz woman. Sharp Memorial, the hospital where both of Jana's parents worked, had paid big bucks to be positioned up front.

Why was she wasting time even thinking about Yvonne Munoz? If the woman wanted Reese McDonald she was welcome to him.

"The auction should start about now," Jana commented, flipping through a pamphlet she'd retrieved from a nearby table. "I can't wait to see Reese McDonald strut his stuff. It's going to make my day. What's the minimum bid for him anyway?" She glanced at the brochure again. "Holy moley…madness."

"How much is he up for?" Twyla asked. "And why are you interested? Are you thinking of bidding on him?"

"Hell, no. The minimum bid is five hundred bucks. Besides, any guy who puts himself up for auction isn't what I want."

"And what do you want?" Twyla asked, looking mildly amused. "I'm beginning to think you don't like men. You haven't been out on a date in how many months?" She began to count her fingers.

"Don't remind me," Jana huffed.

"I should talk. Maybe I will bid on the urban designer and get a little action."

"Whatever."

With that Jana flounced off. Twyla's comments had irritated her for some strange reason. She couldn't decide whether her friend was teasing or deliberately ribbing her. What she did know was that she was not particularly pleased.

With the meal pretty much over with, Jana decided to say hi to her mother, whom she'd not had the time to acknowledge.

Mona was holding court with the women seated around her. Her eyes lit up when she spotted Jana.

"Baby, you and Twyla have done a superb job," she greeted, blowing Jana a kiss. "We were just saying how good the food was and what a wonderful job you did decorating." Mona looked to her colleagues for confirmation. They nodded their agreement, smiled, and went back to chatting.

Mona patted a vacant chair. "Sit down, sweetheart, and join us for a minute. Dr. Kelman was just paged. I doubt that she'll be back."

Jana gratefully sank into the doctor's empty seat. Her feet were beginning to hurt. She should never have bothered to wear the stiletto heels; she should have opted for comfort.

Mona slid a program at her. "What do you think about these men?"

"Oh Mother." Jana poured a glass of water and took her time turning the pages. Ten men of varying ethnicities were up for auction, each profiled on his own page and accompanied by a professional photo. Most were white collar and the few who weren't earned a decent living and held good, solid jobs. Ages ran the gamut from early twenties to late sixties. They all appeared to be in good shape.

The lights dimmed while the wait staff was still picking up the last of the coffee cups and dessert dishes.

Where is Twyla?" Mona whispered. "Kate Farber has another appointment. Have your friend join us."

"Good idea," Jana said, hurrying off to find Twyla.

Jana found her partner in the kitchen talking to the banquet manager. It took a bit of persuading but Twyla finally agreed to join Mona's table. The opportunity to view ten hot men up close and personal was just too much to resist.

The moment they were seated, a Chris Rock impersonator, the MC for the event, began a repertoire of male-bashing jokes. Then Dee Sanford, a popular motivational speaker, took over, thanking everyone for coming and giving the blessing. She mentioned that the proceeds from the brunch and auction would be

donated to Sisters in Transition, an organization providing services for the victims of domestic violence.

The Chris Rock imitator was up again. "Ladies, it's a
booty call," he boomed. "Minimum bids are listed on
those cards in front of you. If the man's hot, break out
that checkbook and put a check beside his name, then
back that check up with money, slide that bid right
into an envelope, and hand it to a volunteer before
the next piece of booty comes on. Remember, it's a silent auction, people. Keep your mouths shut and your
hands writing those checks."

His ribald statement produced more chuckles.

The whole process sounded barbaric to Jana but the
MC though crude was at least funny. She'd heard these
events raised thousands of dollars. Judging by the
hushed anticipation and frantic flipping of pages, the
women here would be shelling out big bucks.

Still, even though things were tough out there, paying money for a date, charity donation or not, was not
to be considered. She had much more on her mind
than finding a man anyway. She had A Fare to Remember to focus on. Once the business was on solid ground
she could turn her attention to her personal situation.

What was she looking for? Someone secure enough
not to try to change her, someone who wouldn't expect her to be Martha Stewart. If he was expecting dinner on the table at a set time, then he needed to learn
how to cook. If he wanted his shirts starched and
ironed, then the neighborhood laundromat could be
quite accommodating. That put a lot of men out of the
running.

"Is there a doctor in the house?" The Chris Rock
wannabe shouted into the microphone, bringing Jana
back to the here and now. "Bachelor number one is

Rexford Stewart, a twenty-nine-year-old internist who loves to fence." He rattled off Rex's statistics and his likes and dislikes, and then repeated the minimum bid. "Put your hands together, ladies. Let the man know he's hot."

And the women were complying. Many were on their feet, catcalling the dark-skinned man with the moustache and skin the texture of velvet. He sauntered out, struck a pose, and continued down the makeshift runway to wild applause.

Dressed in a black tuxedo, he appeared distinguished and classy. The red rose clasped in one hand was given to a young woman seated at Yvonne Munoz's table. The woman's eyes practically bugged out of her head as he blew her a kiss. And the room erupted again.

Hoots, hollers, and catcalls came from everywhere. People were recording entries frantically before the next bachelor came out.

Jana had noted that Reese would be the seventh on-stage. She would deny it if asked, but she could see why he commanded a minimum of five hundred dollars. He was by far the best-looking guy in the auction and his profile was impressive. Anticipating his appearance, she edgily sat through the statistics for a banker, professional baseball player, and popular teacher. She watched a plumber, dressed in nothing more than a pair of boxers and a bow tie, strut his stuff to more cheers and invitations to join the women in bed.

Jana was surprised when Twyla discretely elbowed her. "Why is your mother scribbling down numbers and handing in envelopes?" she asked.

"I don't know. It's a charity event. I suppose she feels compelled to bid."

Twyla didn't seem to buy that explanation. She scratched a spot at the nape of her neck. "What if she's the highest bidder? What will she do with these men?"

"Give them to you," Jana joked. Even so, the thought of her starchy mother having dinner with any of the beefcakes was hilarious, charity event or not. Jana touched Twyla's arm. "Trust me, my mother would never put in a bid that would be considered. She's just attempting to drive the pricing up."

"If you say so." Twyla's eyes were on the stage. She exhaled loudly. "Bachelor number seven's up. You think Yvonne Munoz is having hot flashes?"

Jana looked up to see Councilwoman Munoz looking as if she was in the throes of an orgasm. This was even before Reese's name was mentioned. She wanted to strangle the woman.

The MC was now droning on. "How about a man who designs space for a living? This handsome urban designer's a real catch…"

Reese still hadn't made an appearance but women were already beginning to scribble. Then he walked onstage, all conservative elegance, and Jana's mouth went dry. She just couldn't help staring.

Reese looked like the epitome of the successful businessman in his camel-colored pants, light blue shirt, and navy-striped tie. The whole look complemented his cream-colored skin. A pair of expensive-looking loafers peeked out from under the hem of his slacks. Over his arm he carried the suit jacket.

"Damn! The man's fine," she heard Twyla mutter. Her friend began scribbling on a card.

"Tell me you're not bidding on him," Jana whispered back. "You can't afford five hundred dollars."

"I'll delay paying my rent if I have to."

"You won't."

Jana tried to tug the card away from Twyla but she wouldn't let her.

Reese walked toward the edge of the dais and looked out at the audience. Women went wild. The cabbage roses from the centerpieces were now being tossed at him.

The whole thing was ridiculous. These were supposedly professional women. Had they lost their minds? Jana ventured a look at her mother, who seemed unfazed. Mona was busy tucking a card into an envelope. Jana rolled her eyes. Her mother was taking this fundraising business too seriously; one bid should have been enough.

Three other bachelors followed Reese; one was a man associated with the Rothschild foundation. Interestingly enough, his minimum bid was half of Reese's. Jana was sorely tempted to scribble something on the card in front of her. Not because she was interested, but because it would be an opportunity to let someone from the organization know how she really felt. She quickly dismissed the idea. Taking Twyla with her, she went back to work.

The program moved on to the next stage: awards and presentations. A jazz band played softly in the background, entertaining the crowd. Some of the women danced solo. Meanwhile the results of the silent auction were being tabulated and snippets of conversation drifted over.

"What I could do with bachelor number four."

"No, honey, it's bachelor number seven you want. He's the total package."

And yes, in many ways Reese McDonald was, except he was not for her and she clearly was not for him. Jana continued wandering through the ballroom, making

sure the bar staff had enough mimosas and Bloody
Marys to satisfy an army. She made sure the volunteers
were handing out the chocolate favors she and Twyla
had had made up.

"Look, look, the MC is back," Twyla said when their
paths crossed. "He's got an envelope. Do you think I
might have won?"

"How much did you bid on Reese McDonald?" Jana
asked, curiously.

"Seven hundred bucks."

"That's your rent. Girl, you're crazy. No man's worth
being put out on the street."

"Hush. They're announcing the results."

Twyla took Jana by the elbow and moved her forward toward the stage. Women had begun screaming
as the names of the winners were announced. The ten
bachelors stood in a line, graciously accepting effusive
kisses and stranglehold hugs.

"Come on! Come on! Who won bachelor number sev-
en?" Twyla muttered, two fingers on each hand crossed.

"Hopefully it's not you," Jana said ungraciously.

"Hopefully it is me. One night with him, that's all I
ask."

"You're shameless."

The Chris Rock imitator approached the microphone again. "Mona Davis wins bachelor number
seven. Mona, please come up and claim your man."

"Oh God," Jana said, placing a hand over her face.

"Your mother won," Twyla said, jumping up and
down. "God is good."

Jana glared at her. Her attention returned to the
stage and her mother, who had joined the MC. Mona
was stylishly attired in one of her St. John's suits. She
whispered something in his ear and accepted the card

he handed her. When Mona crossed over to Reese and shook his hand, his expression registered surprise and at the same time admiration. Clearly he hadn't expected to be bid on by an older woman—even so, he now seemed flattered. What would he say if he knew the woman was her mother?

Jana's name was being announced by the MC.

Holy moley.

"You're up," Twyla said, grinning from ear to ear and tugging her forward.

"Jana Davis," the man repeated. "You're needed up here. Bachelor number seven is yours. Lucky man, you've already gotten Mama's approval."

Jana somehow managed to manufacture a smile. She climbed three little steps and joined her mother and Reese on the dais.

Reese stepped forward, prepared to embrace her. Jana held out her cheek for his kiss. Instead of the chaste kiss she expected, he wrapped her in his arms. When Reese's mouth fastened over hers Jana's toes practically curled. Heart pounding, nerve endings twitching, she forgot about the room filled with people. She felt wired, tingly, and alive with feeling. This instantaneous connection was unexplainable, palpable, and very real.

A burst of applause brought her back to the world.

She looked down into the audience and spotted Twyla, a huge smile on her face. Her gaze met and held with Yvonne Munoz's. The councilwoman looked furious. Jana's guess was that Yvonne had been outbid. Twyla, the traitor, she would deal with later.

Right now there were more important issues to deal with, like her traitorous heart.

Trust that damn organ to betray her.

Chapter 10

"Mother, how could you do this to me?"

"Do what to you?" Mona asked, the heels of her Prada pumps making a clip-clop noise against the pavement of the parking lot. She aimed the remote key ring at the door and the Jaguar obligingly unlocked.

"Embarrass me in front of all those people, that's what."

"You appeared to be enjoying some of that embarrassment," Mona said, slipping on practical designer sunglasses. "Did you want to stop by later for dinner, darling?"

Jana wheezed out a breath. "No thanks. I have something to take care of. How much did you bid on that man, anyway?"

Mona narrowed her eyes and looked at her daughter. "Reese McDonald?" she asked, sweetly. "Now why do you need to know that? It was all for a worthy cause." She didn't wait for Jana to respond. She slid into the driver's seat and closed the door.

Jana refused to back off. She crossed her arms and stood her ground.

"If Twyla bid seven hundred dollars, Mother, you had to have bid more than that."

Mona chuckled. "Did I now? Twyla and I had an agreement, darling. Even if she'd won you would still have had that date with Reese."

"How do you figure that?"

"You're a bright girl. You'll figure it out. We both wanted to gauge your reaction."

Jana was slowly beginning to comprehend she'd been duped. There'd been a conspiracy between her mother and the friend she trusted. Some friend. She'd actually thought Twyla was interested in Reese.

Mona put the car in gear and said breezily, "By the way, don't wait too long. Call Reese and set up the date. I'm anxious to hear how it goes."

Jana huffed out another breath. "Maybe I won't go through with it. What difference does it make anyway? The charity's already gotten your money."

"You will," Mona shouted through the open window as she began backing out of the spot. "After that kiss you owe it to yourself."

She drove off leaving Jana speechless.

Reese wrapped up the weekly Sunday call to his brother, Barry, and flipped his cell phone shut. Speaking with Barry always left him with a sad, empty feeling. Talk about a person with no map or plan. So far his brother's search for the right career matched his quest for the perfect wife. And consequently, Barry's life was always in flux. Nothing and no one ever seemed to satisfy him or make him happy.

It would probably get worse now that their father,

Maynard, was dead. Reese had gone to visit the old man after not hearing from him in days. He'd found him dead on the bathroom floor of a stroke, or so the coroner had said. Reese had blamed himself for not checking on his elderly father more often. Maynard's death had made Reese painfully aware of his own mortality and his failings as a son.

Not that Maynard had been such a wonderful dad anyway, but he was the only parental figure Reese really knew. In his clumsy, ineffective way, Maynard had loved his children.

That was just the way it was. Every person that Reese had ever formed an attachment to was eventually taken away. His mother he remembered more as a shadowy figure than a real person. But he did remember her smell because it reminded him of a summer garden.

She too had left him high and dry. Add in the one woman he'd lived with, who had seemed more interested in his wallet than in him. She'd become fed up with his evasiveness after bringing up the "M word" one too many times and had taken up with her gynecologist and moved on.

The opportunity to move to San Diego and design the Lakeview project had come along at just the right time. A change of locale was what he needed badly. It would be therapeutic and help him to work through the loss of both parent and lover.

Enough of that thinking. Good things were on the horizon now. He could feel them. Now that the damn auction was over with, he could concentrate on the plan for the Lakeview Park development.

He'd been pleased with the results of the auction. His date had turned out to be a pleasant surprise: a woman he was actually attracted to. And yes, admit-

tedly he'd been shocked when the elegant, sophisti-
cated, older woman mounted that stage to claim him.
But he'd been fortunate to meet Dr. Davis, Jana's
mother. He couldn't have planned it better if he'd en-
gineered it himself.

Casting a glance at the time on the console of the
Range Rover, Reese realized the lateness of the hour.
He had exactly half an hour to make it back to his
hotel where he was supposed to meet up with his realtor, Jackie Jiminez. Hopefully today they would find
him a place to live.

At the appointed hour, Reese stood out front under
the awning. A few minutes later, Jackie drove up in her
Lexus, sunglasses perched on the bridge of her nose.

She cheerily yelled out of the window, "Good afternoon, my friend," before opening the passenger door
for him. "What a beautiful day. Look how nice you
look." She eyed his attire.

"Thank you," Reese answered. He hadn't had time
to change and was still wearing the outfit he'd worn to
the brunch.

Jackie handed him a stack of property listings she'd
printed out. "I've got at least ten places for you to see
today. Five of them are in City Heights as you requested."

"You don't sound particularly enthused about the
area."

"I don't have to be." Her smile took the sting out of
her words. "You're the one who has to like it."

"What is it you don't like about the neighborhood?"

"How about we head there and you can make an informed decision."

With that she drove off. They remained on the highway for a short time and then headed down University.
Reese noticed the interesting assortment of shops and

restaurants, with signs written in myriad languages. The locale appeared to be a true melting pot and the people on the streets ran the gamut. They appeared to be of various ethnicities—every hue of Latino, Asian, and African.

"The newly emigrated live here," Jackie explained, noticing Reese's interest. She parked the car on a side road and waited for Reese to get out.

"Here's a rental that might be worth looking at. It's reasonable and has a huge backyard for your dogs."

As they walked toward the house, Reese glanced around the neighborhood. The block was well maintained but judging by the vehicles and people coming and going, definitely working class.

Reese followed Jackie into a house with a lockbox on it. He did a quick walk-through, already knowing it wasn't quite what he was looking for. He needed a certain element of charm to fuel his creative juices. And neither were the four other properties they looked at what he had in mind.

"So what do you think so far?" Jackie asked when they were settled in the Lexus again.

"The neighborhood's a work in progress," Reese answered diplomatically. "You were right. It's not exactly what I'm looking for. I'll be spending a lot of hours working and I may be returning late at night. I want to ensure there are no problems with muggings or break-ins. And I'd like to make sure my neighbors are people I have something in common with."

Jackie tapped the steering wheel with her bright red nails. "Golden Hill is a possibility. It's southeast of Balboa Park, and South Park is adjacent. Housing is kind of a hodgepodge, though."

"What exactly does that mean?"

Reese wondered what it was Jackie wasn't saying.

"It's just that you've got a little of everything. There are stately old mansions, quaint bungalows, and apartment buildings, sometimes all lumped together." She gestured to the pile of papers she'd handed him. "Take a look through the lot. There's one huge house for rent that I think you might like. It needs a little TLC but it's charming and has great views of downtown."

"Okay, you convinced me. Take me there." He hadn't glanced at the listing. He was going by gut.

The moment they drove into Golden Hill, Reese was enchanted. It was a cool neighborhood with few pretensions and a mishmash of architectural styles, some competing against each other. He liked that it was eclectic, something for everyone, and he liked the signs of rejuvenation. Others knew it was special. It would be a good time to get in.

The house that Jackie showed him was a massive, rambling thing—Spanish and two stories high. Bedrooms were on the upper floors and French doors led out to individual patios. Some of the wooden floors needed stripping and the tile required regrouting. It needed a good cleaning but overall the possibilities were there.

Despite the bathrooms being outdated and needing remodeling, the faucets were real brass. The pièce de résistance was the master bathroom with its clawfoot tub. Agreed, the square footage was far more than he needed, but he could work with that. There would be plenty of space for his dogs, Luna and Eclipse, to roam. And this way he wouldn't feel guilty like he would leaving them cooped up in some undersized rental while he went to work. They'd love all the nooks and crannies and places to hide.

"What are the rent and the deposit again?" Reese asked as they stood in the old-fashioned kitchen, over-looking sloping lawns and garden beds that needed a good weeding.

Jackie repeated the price. "The owner is willing to go lower if the tenant does a bit of fixing up. She'll pay for the supplies if you provide the labor."

"Sounds like a good deal. Tell her she has a tenant," Reese said, whipping out his checkbook.

"Are you sure you don't want to look at the other properties?" Jackie asked. "There are at least two you might be interested in that wouldn't require work."

"No, this is it. There's something about this house that speaks to me. Plus the dogs will have plenty of space and that's important."

"Okay, then. I'll arrange to have the place cleaned. You can be moved in by next weekend if you'd like."

"I'd like. I'm sick of living out of a suitcase."

Reese followed Jackie back to the Lexus, thinking his life was finally coming together. He'd found a place to live today and he'd even managed to find himself a date. No, correction, a mother had found a date for her daughter.

A date he already liked.

"*¿Que es esto?*"

The inquiry in Spanish came from behind a closed door.

Jana stood on the front steps of the run-down house, holding her ID up to the peephole.

"Jana Davis. Lucy's counselor," she offered up.

"Ah, Lucy's *amiga. Un momento, por favor.*"

There were rustlings and whispers before the bolt

shifted and the security chain slid free. Jana couldn't blame the female on the other end for displaying caution.

Lucy Santana and her aunt lived in the middle of the hood. It didn't get much worse than this. Here drug pushers hung out on the sidewalks and trashcans spilled litter into the streets. At times there was even the occasional dead animal.

Bravely, Jana tried not to inhale the stench of rotting food, reminding herself she was here for Lucy who had been a no-show for her last two counseling sessions. Jana had become increasingly concerned.

The door flew open and an overweight, disheveled woman, balancing a baby on her hip, smiled through crooked teeth.

"*Mamita.* You are Lucia's friend, sí? I am Teresa, Lucia's aunt."

"And I'm Jana Davis, Lucy's friend and counselor. Is she home?"

Lucy's aunt jutted a thumb in the direction of an inner room and rolled her eyes. "I have given up with that one. She refuses to leave the bed. She is starving herself and crying all day over that boy."

"That poor child."

The last time Jana had seen the teenager she was still in the hospital. Lucy had been slowly coming around. She'd appeared bubbly and optimistic, more like her old self.

Now Jana didn't like what she was hearing. Something must have happened to send the teenager back into the dumps.

"But Lucy was given a clean bill of health when she was discharged from Mercy Hospital," Jana said. "I checked on her. Maybe she's having a relapse or just not feeling well."

Teresa's free hand tapped her forehead. "She's not well in the *cabeza,* that girl. She is loco."

"May I see her?"

"Of course you can. She loves you. Talks about you when she talks at all."

Teresa stood aside, letting Jana enter. The baby began wailing. Without apology, Teresa whipped out one gigantic breast and stuck the nipple in the child's mouth. The baby began sucking noisily.

"You go, she will be pleased to see you," Teresa said, shooing Jana down the hallway. "Excuse my mess. I have no time to clean. I am too busy with children and work. Lucia's in the middle room. She must share with my three daughters. They are not home right now."

Jana made her way down a filthy hallway littered with clothing, pacifiers, and broken toys. She knocked on the closed door of the middle room and waited to be acknowledged.

"Go away," a plaintive voice said, after Jana's knocking yielded no response and she'd resorted to banging.

Lucy sounded as if she'd been run over by a Mack truck and left on the side of the street.

"It's Jana," Jana called. "Open up, let me in."

There was dead silence, then nothing.

Jana tried coaxing. "Lucy, come on, sweetie, open up. I miss you."

The door finally swung open and a bedraggled version of Lucy stood before her. The teenager's hair hung in limp clumps. Her face was devoid of makeup, and her empty eyes brimmed with tears that began to spill the moment she saw Jana.

Jana folded the girl into her arms. "It's okay, baby. Talk to me."

Lucy let out a huge gulp. Then the floodgates opened up and tears really began to flow. Jana folded a tissue into the teenager's palm and held her, letting her cry until she'd pretty much worn herself out. Then Jana patted a spot on the unmade bed and guided the girl toward it. "Let's sit and talk. You were feeling much better the last time I saw you. What happened?"

Jana handed Lucy another tissue.

Lucy blew her nose. She joined Jana on the unmade bed and sat, folding and unfolding her hands.

"I told Drew what happened," she said at last. "And he didn't seem to care. He didn't even say he was sorry. He said he was glad."

"That wasn't very nice of Drew, but why are you surprised?" Jana asked. "He made it clear from the beginning that he wasn't interested in the baby. The two of you weren't even dating."

"I know. But I'd expected him to be nicer. I thought the baby might make a difference."

Jana kissed the top of the misguided teenager's head. "Those were *your* expectations, Lucy. Didn't we talk about expectations?"

Lucy sniffed loudly before admitting, "We did. You said it was important for two people to be on the same wavelength and that's why communication is so important."

"You listened."

Jana was surprised by the direct quote. She suddenly realized that Lucy viewed her as something of a role model.

"Are you in love with Drew?" she asked. "Or are you

awed because he's the resident basketball star and has the kind of body you see in those videos?"

Lucy thought about it for a moment. "I used to think I was in love with him, then he became mean."

"And why would you want to be with a mean person?"

"Because no one ever held me the way he did or told me I was beautiful."

Poor child. Jana felt for her. She'd always known Lucy was one of those lost souls looking for love in all the wrong places.

"And so you've locked yourself in your room, refusing to eat because Drew has shown his true colors. Now what's that going to accomplish?"

Lucy hung her head.

"It's not going to change anything, is it? Drew's still dating Kendra so you need to move on with your life. Find someone who appreciates and values you."

"I suppose I should," Lucy admitted as if unable to believe such a boy existed. "It hurts me to think I no longer have my baby to love."

Jana bit back the retort that came to mind. "I am sorry for your loss, Lucy. There will be other children in your future. With time, hopefully you can put this behind you."

Lucy looked like she was about to break down in tears again and Jana placed an arm around her shoulders. "Go clean up, honey, and I'll take you to dinner at my friend Carmen's home. She has kids your age. It's time you met some new people. Decent people."

"Does Carmen have a son?" Lucy asked, a hint of the old brightness in her voice.

"Three. And Roberto is exactly your age."

"Cool. Then maybe I will go to dinner with you."

Jana hugged the irrepressible teen. "Spoken like the young woman I remember. Now go make yourself pretty."

Chapter 11

Reese's finger traced a path across his revised plan. "I was thinking," he said to Bruce Rothschild, "this green might be improved with a fountain or two."

"What green?" Bruce asked distractedly, the thumb of one hand stabbing the buttons of his cell phone.

"The square in the middle of the common areas. The one we agreed would be open to the public. I was thinking cobblestone walkways leading to the piers might be an interesting concept."

Bruce glanced at Reese over the top of his half-moon glasses. "Piers or dock space?" He brought the cell phone to his ear. "Dammit, Seth's line is still busy."

"Fishing piers," Reese patiently explained, his fingers pointing to the design spread out on the table. "Here and here. The green is public space and so are the fishing piers. Those are the concessions we agreed on so that these folks would calm down and cooperate with us. We need to get those final permits, remember? We discussed throwing them a bone. I've modified the design to include biking paths and a botanical garden—that's supposed to make up for leveling the community center."

Bruce shoved the cell phone into his jacket pocket. His blank stare indicated he might have forgotten the conversation. "We're under no obligation to provide any extras. You created affordable housing and that should be enough. Don't let them bully us."

Holding his ground, Reese smiled affably. "Affordable means different things to different people. Homes starting in the high three hundreds are not affordable to folks barely making it."

Bruce crossed over to the table where the plans were spread. "So where are these public spaces?"

Reese used the same finger to trace a path again while carefully explaining his vision.

"Forget about it," Bruce huffed. "That's wasted space that could be revenue-producing. Why give up the income the dockage and retail stores would bring? These people are blowing smoke, they'll soon get over it."

"The community's already picketing," Reese warned. "Things could get difficult if they continue, and we're on a tight deadline as it is."

Reese hoped his anger wasn't visible. Bruce's last comment didn't help either. Reese himself was "one of these people," or had been, until he'd been fortunate enough to earn an advanced degree in a field that made decent money.

"So they're picketing. Change is hard, they'll adjust."

It would be best to keep his irritability to himself. It would serve no useful purpose.

"Be that as it may," he said, "goodwill goes a long way. A compromise of some kind will make the folks feel they were listened to. There's also the big picture to consider. Our plans for Lakeview Park will garner lots of media interest. Curiosity alone will drive business. Whenever you create a new hot spot revenues will follow. Look at South Beach. The Gaslamp District right here is proof enough."

"People need to feel safe," Bruce announced, but Reese could tell a jingling register had his interest piqued.

Bruce's cell phone chose that moment to play one of those silly tunes that sounded like "Money, money, money." He flipped open the phone, glanced at the incoming number, and bellowed into the mouthpiece. "Well it's about time, Seth."

Then, glancing at Reese, he stalked out into the hall to conduct his business in private.

Somehow, someway, Reese had to get through to the man. These were his people.

Mona let it slip that she'd bid close to double the minimum to make sure she won Reese McDonald. Jana thought her mother was crazy. No man was worth anywhere near that much money.

"Why him, Mother?" she challenged after almost having a cow. "There were ten men strutting their stuff. From what I could gather, most of them came cheaper."

Mona then laughingly said, "Something tells me Reese is worth it. And after that rather lengthy display you two put on, I just might be right. I'd like to see you married and settled down."

"Oh Mother." Jana had then quickly ended the conversation. It was Mona's way of trying to exert control and bring order to Jana's life. Since her mother had already spent that much money she might as well get a free meal out of it.

Twyla soon threw a damper on that thought. She reminded Jana that since she was the one responsible for setting up the date, there was a good likelihood she'd end up with the tab. The person who asked inevitably paid.

Might as well get it over with then. It was going on two weeks since the auction and brunch, and she still couldn't bring herself to call Reese. She grappled with her feelings. On some level he'd let her down. She'd been expecting more from Reese at the meeting. She'd hoped that he would find some way to save the community center and the building would be left intact. But he hadn't.

Jana's roommate, Winston, a male flight attendant, was out of town. Tonight she had the apartment to herself and was looking forward to a relaxing evening.

She opened the newspaper and checked the events listed for the upcoming weekend. An outdoor festival of art and jazz on the waterfront caught her attention. Yes, that might work. No stress and no pressure. It would be a good way to fulfill her obligation without getting stuck across a dinner table with Reese.

Before she could lose her courage, Jana picked up the phone and punched in the number written on the card her mother had handed her. She took a deep breath, composing herself.

"McDonald," a male voice snapped.

"Reese?"

"Who is this?"

Did he sound annoyed or simply distracted? It was hard to tell.

"It's Jana."

He chuckled. "It's taken you long enough to call me. I've been waiting."

"Better late than never," Jana retorted. "I'm calling you now, aren't I?"

"So you are. What's up?"

"What are you doing on Sunday afternoon?"

"I'll have to check my social calendar," he joked. "What did you have in mind?"

Jana told him about the street fair and about the street musicians and artists who would be there. "It's an annual happening," she said, "and very well attended."

"Sounds like fun," Reese said agreeably. "Where do you live, anyway?"

"No, where do *you* live?" Jana countered. "I'm asking you on this date. I'm picking you up."

"On Golden Hill, and I was only asking because I thought maybe you'd like to join me jogging. I'm thinking of heading out. You seem athletic enough. We could meet on a corner somewhere and afterward you could see my new place and tell me what you think."

Talk about being put on the spot. The ironic thing was that she had thought about running that evening but hadn't been motivated. And running did help to keep her stress level down. She would never have guessed they had this activity in common. And yes, there was something about the man that drew her, as infuriatingly obnoxious as he sometimes could be.

Now someone was conspiring big-time. Golden Hill was her neighborhood. With her luck Reese might even live next door.

"My apartment's on Orchard," she offered. "On Golden Hill as well," she added, in case he didn't know.

"Perfect. Let's meet in, say, twenty minutes. Any suggestions as to where we should meet? Usually I run for an hour or so—think you can keep up?"

How nervy of him. But he'd tossed down the gauntlet and by damn she would pick it up, her competitive spirit being what it was. She mentioned a popular coffee shop and they agreed to meet there in half an hour.

Reese did a series of stretches and bends on the sidewalk, warming up while he waited for Jana to put in an appearance. He spotted her sauntering down the sidewalk, earphones on. He used that time to slowly assess her.

Jana's bushy, blond-tipped curls were partially stuffed under a navy cap with a low bill. She had on navy athletic shorts and a white T-back top that stopped an inch or two above her waistband, revealing an ample bit of toned flesh. She looked ready to run. The Walkman and water bottle strapped around her waist indicated she wasn't exactly a novice.

She was by no means what he would describe as skinny. Jana was nicely proportioned with a high, ample butt. She had strong, athletic legs and a stomach you could bounce a quarter off of. There wasn't an ounce of excess fat on her anywhere.

Her skin tone was butterscotch. Her smoky eyes mesmerized him, especially when he pushed one of her buttons and they turned steel gray. X-rated thoughts came to mind just gazing at those legs striding toward him. She was still listening to her headphones and oblivious that he was watching.

Reese began jogging toward her. Jana didn't see him until he was almost on top of her. He waved a hand in front of her face and a slow smile made her look less serious. Now it was her turn to assess him.

A flicker of something he didn't know how to interpret registered in those exotic gray eyes of hers. She removed her headphones and grinned at him, looking him up and down in wonder.

"Nice to see you showing some skin and looking more relaxed," she said, winking. "Those chinos and starched cotton shirts were getting awfully old."

He had that coming. Tit for tat and all that. Jana was getting back at him for all the snide comments he'd made about her funky clothing.

"Any suggestions as to where we should head to?" he asked.

"Depends on what you have in mind. My preference is to jog by the older mansions and head toward the high school. There's a big ball field where I do laps. It's well lit after dark. Most people in the neighborhood bring their dogs there to run."

"Sounds like it's right up my alley. Let's get going, then."

For the next fifty minutes or so, they jogged up and down several blocks that were close to his house, but he never once mentioned it. They passed sprawling mansions set back from the road and beautifully tended gardens. Reese could only imagine what the neighborhood must have been like in its heyday. Based on the construction going on around him, it was on its way back.

While heading for the schoolyard, they passed joggers, cyclists, and people walking their dogs. After completing three laps around the ball field, Reese decided to call time out. He jutted a thumb toward the bleachers. "What do you say we cool down and catch our breath?"

Jana nodded her agreement and began running in place. She handed him her water bottle. Reese took a big swig. Beads of sweat glistened on Jana's forehead and trickled down her neck. He longed to reach over, and with his fingers trace the path of one of those rivulets. Better not. Who knew how Jana would react?

They began walking slowly toward the bleachers. On the second tier they sat, not touching. Jana stared out onto the ball field where parents were pitching to children swinging wildly. Reese found something magical about this time of evening when you could still see without the aid of artificial light, and the fragrance of a thousand blossoms seemed magnified. Dusk provided hope of a new tomorrow.

"What are you thinking?" Reese asked. There were a million thoughts reflected in those gun-smoke eyes.

"About how tranquil this time of evening is. Everything seems so serene as we settle in for the night."

She was mirroring his thoughts exactly.

"I couldn't have said it better. What are you doing for dinner?"

She clearly hadn't given it much thought. She cocked her head, considering. "I'm definitely not cooking if that's what you're asking. I'll probably have takeout."

He'd been handed a gift. Only a fool or an uninterested man wouldn't accept it.

"Can I persuade you to join me?" Reese asked. "I can throw a couple of steaks on the barbecue or hot dogs and hamburgers if you prefer."

"I don't eat meat," Jana answered, sounding horrified by his proposal.

Oops! He'd have to recover quickly or the opportunity would be gone. "Okay, so I'll barbecue you mushrooms, corn, potatoes, whatever you'd like."

"I'd like," Jana said, pretending to sniff under her armpits. "You'll just have to put up with my BO."

"A woman's natural scent is a big turn on. Besides, I doubt I smell like roses."

That produced a big smile. Jana seemed to be enjoying her time with him. They were okay together as long as they didn't talk about Lakeview Park.

"We should start walking and take advantage of what's left of the light," Reese suggested, extending a hand to help Jana up.

"You live close to here?" she asked suspiciously.

"Don't you?"

"Yes, not too far."

"So there isn't a problem. After we eat I can drop you off or walk you home, whichever you prefer."

Jana said nothing.

Reese still held on to her hand. The good thing was she was letting him. Side by side, they walked the six long blocks to the house he'd rented.

Reese slowed down before the huge Spanish hacienda, with the terra cotta tile roof, set back from the road. At one time the building was grand—no more. Now it needed major work.

"This is my home," he announced, waving Jana through a rusty wrought iron gate and up a weed-strewn path where flowers struggled to survive. The front door was an ornate, hand-carved thing and the knob real brass.

He bent over and slid the key out from under the mat. That set off the rambunctious twosome inside barking.

"Shut up, you old hounds," Reese called to his dogs, good-naturedly. "We have company. I want you on your best behavior." To Jana he said, "Please tell me you like animals, mine are not very well trained."

"I love animals," she hastened to reassure him, and

seemed unfazed by the barking of Luna and Eclipse, thus earning herself another point in his book.

"What kind of pooches are they? I've always wanted another dog," Jana commented. "I have Bourbon, but he's really my parents' dog, unfortunately my apartment complex will not allow pets."

They'd entered the foyer and were almost knocked over by the two yapping Goldens who came bounding at them.

"Down, Eclipse and Luna. Mind your manners. If you don't behave, our guest might never come back."

Jana raised an eyebrow but did not comment. She reached over and scratched each dog behind the ear. Then, as if she'd hypnotized them, one by one they rolled onto their backs.

What had Reese meant by her "not coming back"? This was a one-time thing, an invitation she'd accepted on impulse. Yet Reese had made it sound as if he wanted to make inviting her over a habit.

"Well, I never," he huffed, nudging first Luna then Eclipse with a sneaker-clad foot.

The dogs just laid there waiting until Jana got on her knees and began roughhousing with them. After a while she stood and slowly gazed about her. Reese's place didn't have a whole lot of furniture, but what pieces there were, were tasteful and complemented the Spanish-style ambience.

The living room she'd now wandered into, followed by the dogs at her heels, held a distressed leather sectional with comfortable ottomans. Reese's gigantic entertainment center was home to a monstrous television set and trophies lined up by size on the shelves.

She followed Reese into a formal dining room that was empty of furniture. The tile floors needed a good polishing but could be beautiful again. Jana stopped in front of a picture window with a padded seat and looked out on a circular patio holding wrought iron outdoor furniture.

"You did well for yourself," she said. "This is quite the find."

"Thank you. I prefer things a bit more orderly but truthfully I haven't had time. I'm not done showing you everything," he said, heading off and expecting her to follow.

Reese led the way into an old-fashioned kitchen with flagstone floors and beamed ceilings. Copper pots, probably left by the previous owner, hung from the rafters. There were double steel sinks and a bar in the corner. A counter, flanked by Mission-style chairs, ran the length of the room. A booth, the kind you climbed into, overlooked an overgrown garden heavy with roses in various stages of bloom. Windows, the mullioned kind, and the type you pushed out, let in the cooling evening breeze.

Reese's house was charming and old-fashioned and Jana had fallen in love with it.

"What's upstairs?" she asked, as the Goldens sniffed and licked at her ankles.

"Three bedrooms, two baths, and a quaint room right under the eaves that I plan on turning into an office."

"I'd love to see them," Jana said impulsively.

Reese's eyebrows wiggled but he quickly schooled his expression. "Sure."

He led the way up a winding staircase with a banister that could use some elbow grease—translation: sanding and polishing.

On the landing she stepped onto an aging, but what

might once have been expensive, Persian runner. Jana didn't have time to fully admire it. Reese had already ducked into a room on the right. It was painted Wedgwood blue and held boxes in an orderly stack he must still be unpacking. The one piece of furniture was a comfortable armchair. Jana walked over to the closed French doors. Streams of golden light poured in from outside, dappling the mosaic-tile floors. It was all very enchanting.

"May I?" she asked, her hand on the brass knob.

"Of course you may."

She threw the door wide and stepped out. Reese followed her onto a narrow platform with a railing encircling it.

"It's a widow's walk," he explained. "Usually found in New England homes along the coast and designed so that women who had husbands at sea could look out to see if they were coming home."

"That's an interesting combo of architecture; I guess the owner couldn't make up his mind. It's still sad to think of a woman looking out to sea for her husband. It doesn't conjure up a happy picture."

"Not meant to, I think."

Time to change the subject to something more uplifting. Jana leaned over the railing to get a better view of the sloping lawns and untidy gardens. The lights in buildings in downtown San Diego, although there was really no formal downtown, were beginning to pop on. It was a beautiful sight from this vantage point.

Jana inhaled the heady fragrance of roses and let her imagination go wild. She'd always wanted to live in a place like this, perfect in its imperfection.

"Those roses are to die for," she said.

She could feel Reese behind her, smell the musk of

his skin. His hands were on the railing, trapping her. He blew a soft, whispery breath against her nape and she shivered.

"What you smell are roses, jasmine, and thyme."

Jana's entire body tightened. There was a flutter in her gut she couldn't identify. Reese was too close for comfort and there was no escaping him unless she was deliberately rude.

She needed space to sort out her jumbled feelings about the man. In so many ways Reese attracted her, yet there was that side that repelled her. No, repel was too strong a word, he scared her. It was all that sinew, muscle, and musky masculine odor that overwhelmed her and jumbled her thinking. Reese made her feel feminine yet powerful and at times even tongue-tied, something she'd never been. Jana turned in Reese's arms. The second she did so she knew she'd made a huge mistake.

She came up flush against his chest, her fisted hands connecting with the solid wall that was his chest. Reese's corded arms steadied her. Heated flesh met heated flesh. Her nose was only inches away from his chest, a chest that was tinged burgundy with exertion. Jana smelled heat and desire as Reese's muscular thighs grazed hers. His head dipped and his lips claimed her mouth.

Jana swayed against him and her mouth opened up. Reese's tongue probed and entered in a slow yet insistent exploration. His hands left the railing to settle on her butt. When Reese tightened his grip on her, Jana could feel his rapidly swelling erection. He was not the kind of man you toyed with. She had no idea how things had gotten so quickly out of control.

It had to be stopped before both of them regretted

this. Then Reese kissed her again and for the life of her, she couldn't summon the strength to pull away. Another wave of pure pleasure took over and she kissed him back with abandon, letting her tongue circle and probe the sweet concaves of his mouth. Once in a while, in a synchronized dance, their tongues met.

"Shouldn't we see to dinner?" Jana gasped against Reese's mouth.

"Why, are you starving?"

She wanted to say yes, but it wasn't food that she sought.

Reese was grinding into her, and she was letting him. She pulled the T-back top up to expose her bare midriff. She held Reese's head between her palms allowing him to nip at her naked skin. He used the tip of his tongue to trace moist patterns across her stomach and encircle her bellybutton. The overt message was that he wanted her.

His hands yanked at the athletic top and crawled under her sports bra. His slender fingers teased her nipples and made her feel like she would jump out of her skin. She was whirring quickly out of control and she wasn't even on an official date with the man. She did not want him to think she was easy.

"Reese," Jana pleaded. "I'm sorry, but we can't take this further."

"Why not?"

"Because I don't want to."

It was all she needed to say. He released her immediately and turned his back in an effort to regain control. Jana could hear his heavy breathing.

"I'm sorry," she said, placing a hand on his back.

He flinched as if she'd seared him.

In a throaty voice he finally said, "There's no reason

to be. I'm the one that's sorry." Speaking seemed an effort. "I've behaved like a cad."

It was an old-fashioned expression and one her father often used. It endeared him to her.

"You did not. It just happened," Jana said.

"I shouldn't have let it. I'll go downstairs and start dinner now. Would you like to help me?"

"You betcha I will."

And just to make it clear that all was forgiven, Jana winked at him.

Chapter 12

"Save Lakeview Park! Save Lakeview Park!" the people on the sidewalk in front of the Rothschild building chanted. They continued to circle.

Pedestrians stopped to ask what was going on and the picketers loudly and vocally shared their feelings, garnering the support and sympathy of the public. Meanwhile a camera crew was busy filming and a reporter interviewed the loudest of the crowd and individuals with the biggest beef or the loudest mouth.

A van remained parked illegally in a NO PARKING zone. It had a bright red insignia on its side and was from one of the better-known television stations. Ratings must be poor.

Bruce Rothschild spotted the group the moment he stepped out of the covered parking lot and headed toward his building. Come hell or high water he planned on using that main entrance.

He would brazen it out. No cowering for him. What could they do? Even so, he pushed buttons on his cell phone frantically, yelling into the mouthpiece the moment his assistant answered.

"Get someone from City Hall on the phone now. Find out if these people out front have a permit to picket. If the answer is no, call the police and have them arrested."

"But Mr. Rothschild…"

"But Mr. Rothschild nothing. Just do it."

Bruce was already several minutes late for his meeting with Reese McDonald. The designer was beginning to irritate him; he was much too sympathetic to these people's cause. Bruce couldn't let that happen. He would not under any circumstances bow to pressure.

This whole ruckus was unnecessary. What did these people want—blood? Instead of making a fuss they should be kissing his behind. Lakeview Park was smack in the middle of one of the city's worst neighborhoods. It had become a haven for drug addicts and the unsavory. He was the one investing money to revitalize a neglected property that no one else would touch.

The ramshackle building they were going on about was a poor excuse for a community center. All it did was shelter undesirables and give them an excuse to not find work.

One of the picketers spotted him coming. The chanting soon changed. "Bruce Rottenschild has to go!" the crowd crooned, their voices swelling. "Bruce Rottenschild has to go!"

What looked to be a boiled egg was thrown directly at his head. Bruce ducked, watching as the thing hit the pavement and crumbled into yellow and white pieces.

Enough was enough. He lost it. His finger stabbed the air. "What is it with you people?" he shouted. "You can't appreciate a good thing when it happens. Are you so conditioned to living in a slum?"

The crowd went wild. They converged on him. A microphone was stuck under his nose and a flashbulb went off in his face. Bruce's temper flared as a picketer broke free from the line and approached him.

"Hey, Brucy, pussy, so why can't you just build us another community center and get us out of the slum?"

"Yeah, why?"

Why indeed? The truth was the types of residents and vendors the organization hoped to attract did not include the likes of these people. The goal was to attract those with spending power.

"The budget doesn't permit it," Bruce snapped.

"Bull!" the man shouted. "If you can spring for fishing piers and a botanical garden, you can give the tired community center a facelift. It should cost you far less. Give up one of your fancy boutiques and make us happy."

"Yeah," the rest of the crowd crowed. "Yeah! Make us happy!"

They were closing in on him, and that damn microphone was still in his face. Flashbulbs were going off from afar as well as too close for comfort. He was trapped.

With a great deal of relief, Bruce heard sirens approaching. Some of the picketers scattered but others held their ground.

A guttural male voice boomed through a bullhorn. "Break this up and move along! Come on, people, let's do this peaceably."

An apple core hit one of the cop cars and what looked to be someone's sneaker smashed into another. The police were out of their vehicles in a flash. They bellowed a series of warnings through the megaphone, and more people scattered. Those who stayed were now sitting on the sidewalk holding hands and forming a human chain. They continued to chant.

"Brucy, pussy, Brucy, pussy."

The reporters were having a field day walking amongst them and shoving microphones in the faces of those most vocal. The cops, mindful of appearing ineffectual, began handcuffing a few and dragging them toward their vehicles.

The demonstration, if that's what it was supposed to be, had turned into a mess.

Bruce decided it was time to hightail it out of there and fast. Most likely his face would be smeared all over the evening news. Rhonda Watson needed to be called in for damage control.

Bruce Rothschild had kept Reese waiting for what had to be a good forty-five minutes. Reese was now becoming concerned. It was unlike the developer to be late. Usually Bruce arrived at the appointed hour, barking a series of directives before racing off to his next meeting.

Reese normally arrived at Rothschild headquarters early for work. His days started at seven. It was an old habit, one learned from a brief stint in the air force. There was something about the peacefulness of the early hour that set the tone for the rest of the day. The world had not yet invaded. He was at his most productive and creative at this time of day.

Already this morning he'd made several adjustments to the plans for Lakeview Park, changes he needed to discuss with Bruce. They needed to get back to the community with an update and soothe the already-ruffled feathers.

The wall clock indicated that it was now going on nine. Very late for Bruce. Their meeting had been set up for eight and the discussion was to have taken place over coffee, at least coffee for Bruce, tea for Reese. But

Reese had not seen or heard anything from the developer and that concerned him. He'd give it another ten minutes, then he would try ringing Bruce's cell phone.

A combination of raised voices and sirens could be heard from outside. Up until then Reese had been oblivious to the sounds around him. He'd been focusing on how he would present his side of the argument. He crossed the floor of the conference room—a tiny corner had been converted to office space for him—and stared out the window.

What he saw set him into motion. Several people seated on the concrete sidewalk were being handcuffed and thrown into the back of police cars. Some of these people were as old as his father, had he lived, some even older.

Concerned, Reese rushed from the room. On his way out to the lobby, he ran into several harried-looking clerical workers chatting amongst themselves.

"What's going on?" Reese asked one huddled group.

"The picketers got out of control," one of them said.

"They had no permit," another explained. "They began abusing Mr. Rothschild and he had them arrested."

"He didn't just have them arrested," interrupted the first person who had spoken. "He was provoked. Some old guy tossed an egg at him, then rotten fruit at one of the police cars, and that set the cops into motion. You don't mess with them boys in blue, they get brutal."

"Thanks," Reese said, hurrying off, thinking: no wonder Bruce was late.

By the time he got to the lobby and looked out through the glass front, the melee had drawn a crowd of curiosity seekers. Enough cops had been called in to stop a small revolution. Some were wearing protective gas masks. It didn't take a rocket scientist to figure out what the next step would be.

Rothschild Security, in actuality two burly men, clad in drab-gray suits with walkie-talkies, flanked Bruce. The developer, looking like he was about to explode, came hurrying in. His red cheeks indicated his agitation. A cameraman followed closely on his heels. The man was stopped at the revolving front doors. He now aimed the camera at the glass walls.

Bruce would certainly not be in the mood this morning to deal with Reese or his plans for Lakeview Park.

Reese remained in the lobby, watching more of the picketers scatter. The more obstinate ones remained firmly entrenched, chanting at the top of their lungs. The threat of tear gas didn't seem to faze them. The police warnings came through the megaphones loud and clear. The demonstrators ignored them. They too were determined to be heard and get attention from the media.

A horrifying thought occurred to Reese: what if Jana was amongst these people? He hoped for her sake she was not.

Rhonda Watson, Bruce's public relations executive, came hurrying by. She didn't seem to notice him at first. Her attention was on the stack of papers she was hurriedly flipping through. She must have been dispatched to make a public statement and smooth over any damage Bruce might have caused. He didn't envy the woman her job. He felt sorry for her.

"Hey, Rhonda," Reese said, peeling himself off the wall where he was leaning, watching the action.

Rhonda's black-rimmed spectacles did a bit of a jiggle. She seemed flustered but pulled herself together even managing a stiff smile.

"How are you, Reese?"

"Well, thanks. What's going on?"

"I don't have time to talk. Maybe later. The people at the Lakeview Community Center are acting up."

"Perhaps I can help," Reese offered.

Rhonda tapped the toe of a sensible pump and thought for a second. Did the woman ever loosen up? "Tell you what," she said. "You come outside with me. I'll introduce you as the designer responsible for rejuvenating Lakeview Park. We'll play the race card to our advantage and garner the television audiences' attention. My guess is they're already in sympathy with the poor and elderly who were hauled away. Our joint appearance and my comments are going to make the viewers rethink their position."

Reese was outraged. He wanted no part of it.

"Rhonda," he said, "I'm not sure I want to participate in that kind of overt manipulation of public opinion. It would be much more effective if we could tell the reporters what solutions have been offered. Better to make the Lakeview community sound unreasonable."

"Mr. Rothschild doesn't want me to," Rhonda explained, shooting down the idea. "He said the plans were not finalized and anything we say publicly we'll have to honor. He doesn't want to be railroaded into anything."

Reese paused and took a breath. It didn't make sense that an organization with a reputation for developing run-down properties would be so shortsighted. They could easily turn the press to their advantage. If they put the right spin on it, the Lakeview Park development could be viewed as the hottest property around, and when completed the new "in" place to be. The time was now and it wouldn't take a fortune in marketing money to get public attention.

This must not be the first time the developer faced opposition. Bruce had to be shrewd enough to know that if he got the community on his side things would go a heck of a lot smoother. Yet he seemed reluctant to give an inch. Perplexing.

"On second thought Rhonda," Reese said, "sounds like you have things well in hand. You're perfectly capable of facing the good folks of Lakeview alone."

"No, she's not," a male voice that was vaguely familiar interjected, coming up quietly behind them. "Bruce wants you out there standing right next to Rhonda. He says you're to answer questions if you're asked, but don't make any promises. Revisions to your design are still pending approval and have not yet been authorized."

Reese turned to see Seth Bloom standing practically on top of them. Reese still wasn't sure exactly what the man did. What's more he didn't like him one bit. Reese choked back what he really wanted to say and smiled pleasantly.

"If you don't mind, Seth, I'd rather get directives from the man himself and not you. Good luck, Rhonda."

Still smiling pleasantly, though he was seething inside, Reese sauntered away.

"Jana, your community center's on the television. And oh, girl, the peeps are angry. There's police and everything."

Jana had been giving her closet a much-needed cleaning out, but now Winston's excited shouts got her attention. Not that she could make out his words over the rukus on TV.

"What are you taking about?" she shouted back, sticking her head out from the walk-in closet.

Winston came flouncing into the bedroom. He was wearing drawstring linen pants and a formfitting pea green T-shirt. He had moisturizer on his face and strips of cotton between his toes. He looked like he might have been giving himself a pedicure. Since he had a couple of days off between trips, pampering himself pretty much came with that territory.

Winston was gay and made no apologies for his sexuality. His unshakeable self-confidence was what Jana admired most about her roommate, that and his in-your-face honesty.

"Better come quickly," Winston jabbered, tugging on Jana's hand. "You'll want to see this. Your community center is news. Those folks are angry. Girl, you need to see people being hauled off in handcuffs. It's not pretty."

Jana dumped a handful of clothing on the closet floor, which she'd been considering donating to some worthwhile charity, and went racing into the living room where the television was.

A reporter was on-screen talking in excited tones. Jana turned up the volume and tried to follow. There was something about picketing and about the gathering turning unruly. She heard something about tear gas being used, and shuddered. A picture flashed across the monitor. It wasn't pretty.

Lottie Addison, an old lady who had to be eighty if she was a day, was being handcuffed and thrown into the back of a police car. So was Hugh Pilgrim, a homeless man who was too proud to admit it, so everyone went along with his story that he lived with his granddaughter.

The picture now changed, shifting from the reporter to the mouthpiece for the Rothschild organization: their stuffy PR woman, Rhonda Watson. Rhonda

droned on and on, saying something about it being un-
lawful to picket without a permit, and that the residents of the surrounding areas of Lakeview Park were
being unreasonable. She went on and on about the
benefits that could be reaped by beautifying the park
and that the result would be a lowered crime rate.

And although it seemed as if her little citizen group
had gotten way out of hand, Jana felt like throwing a
shoe at the television screen. How dare she? How on
earth could an African American stand there mouth-
ing platitudes when her people, those less fortunate
than she, were being thrown out on the street under
the guise of gentrification?

Rhonda Watson had the nerve to talk about lower-
ing the crime rate. Did she have any idea what would
happen when those basketball courts got torn up and
the community center leveled? Did she have any idea
what it was like to lose your home, as would inevitably
happen once the surrounding properties were bought
up? Did she know what it was like to be poor and downtrodden with no outlet for your angst? The woman
needed a serious reality check.

A picture of Reese flashed across the screen. The reporter introduced him as "the urban designer
brought in from Baltimore." Winston, whom she'd almost forgotten about, gasped and stabbed a finger in
the air.

"Now that is what I call one fine man," he said, strik-
ing a pose. "That would be a total waste if he's
straight."

"He is straight," Jana said, shooting Winston an
amused look. "That's the urban designer I've been
talking about. The visionary for Lakeview Park," she
added sarcastically.

"Oh my." Winston fanned himself. "Mother Mona has good taste, no wonder she bought him for you." Winston did a chicken neck, his eyes practically bugging out of his head as he jerked his neck back and forth. "You cancel your date, girlfriend, and I'm stepping in."

"Shush, Winston! I can't hear what the reporter is saying."

Crossing over to the television, Jana turned the volume up yet another notch.

"We've tried reaching Mr. McDonald for his statement but he's not taking calls," the reporter said. "Several questions come to mind. Will the Lakeview Community Center remain intact? How long will the elderly and infirm stay in jail? Most are too poor to raise bail on their own. If you are interested in helping out those incarcerated, contributions are being taken. Citizens wishing to make donations may call the toll-free number flashing at the bottom of your television screen: 866-OUR-PARK." The reporter then loudly repeated the number.

Then the news quickly shifted to another tragedy.

Winston forgotten, Jana stood there dumbfounded, the remote in her hand. Determined to help out in the only way she could think of, she went off to find her cell phone and call her father.

Bail money was badly needed. And as much as she hated to ask her parents for assistance, she couldn't let her friends languish in jail.

Chapter 13

It took almost three days before the folks who were arrested were bailed out. Jana's dad had come through, contributing several thousand dollars to the fund. Meanwhile, she spent endless hours at the community center trying to soothe ruffled feathers and calm everyone down.

Between Jana's full-time job at Planned Parenthood and her secondary job putting together events for A Fare to Remember, plus her volunteer work at the Lakeview Park Community Center, she was worn out. But she couldn't just turn her back on the people she'd been helping. They needed to be able to vent their anger at someone who would listen and be sympathetic.

The majority were outraged because Lottie Addison, following her release from jail, was supposedly hospitalized. There were rumors the eighty-five-year-old woman had been mistreated while incarcerated. It was said she had heart palpitations, then that rumor soon changed to a full-fledged heart attack.

Some felt that "Tom," the designer, meaning Reese, had betrayed them—that he had been vocal at the meetings but now, when it really mattered, no one had heard from him. What about the promises he'd made to them? The concessions they'd been offered?

Those resigned to being pushed around just shrugged, and mumbled something about his behavior being typical. They urged everyone to get over it and move on.

And Jana, well, she was angry and resentful. She too felt that Reese had let them down. Her disappointment was such that she couldn't even get excited when Lucy Santana phoned declaring herself in love. Things were going well between Lucy and Carmen's seventeen-year-old son, Roberto. The two had taken one look at each other that evening over dinner, and Drew Nelson had been relegated to history. A good thing too since Drew had been one of the young people carted off to jail.

Now Jana was faced with a dilemma as the weekend approached. There was still that matter of her date with Reese. Truthfully she felt like canceling. If she was seen with Reese it would be viewed as betraying her community-center friends. Ah, what to do. How would he explain what had happened at Rothschild headquarters and why things had gotten so out of hand? And to think she'd started to like the man and thought he had scruples.

It occurred to Jana that she might not be giving him a fair shake. Reese McDonald was not the Rothschild organization; he was simply contracted by the company. He had a job to do, just as she had her job to do. At times you didn't agree with your employer and either you bit your tongue or spoke up, but eventually you went along with the program.

But Reese had to know, after talking to the neighborhood people, how important this center was to them. For many it was the only outlet they had, their one source of recreation. The center also provided them fellowship and contact with the outside world.

As Jana was on the highway heading home, her cell phone rang. Using one hand, she fumbled through her purse, found her earpiece, and popped it into her ear.

"Hello."

"Jana?"

She recognized the voice instantly. Her heart did a little dance or maybe it was her blood pressure that had skyrocketed. She felt a little dizzy.

"Yes, this is she."

"It's Reese. I'm checking in with you, wanting to confirm we're on for Sunday. Are we?"

Here was her opportunity to cancel the date. She could come up with some excuse and maybe push him off for a bit.

"Yes, we're on," she said grudgingly.

"Well don't sound so excited."

"Where have you been?" Jana tossed back, not because she was upset he hadn't called before, although she was, but because his disappearance was cowardly. He must have known that the gentrification of Lakeview Park and the imprisonment of these poor people was on everyone's tongue. Headlines had been made and the arrest of the old and infirm had not endeared the Rothschild organization to the public.

"Working," Reese said, then more teasingly. "Did you miss me?"

Jana snorted and decided to let it go. "Given recent events, someone from your organization should have hightailed it to the center to smooth things over. What about that PR woman, Rhonda Watson? No one has seen hide nor hair of her except for on television. A public apology would have gone a long way."

Silence initially greeted her comment. "You've made your point," Reese said at last. "I've attempted to talk to Bruce about the situation but he's been tied up. We're meeting in a few minutes and I'll broach the issue again. Maybe I'll have something good to report on Sunday, providing you still want to go out with me." The last was said playfully.

"Who's picking whom up?" Jana countered.

"Is that a yes, then? How about I pick you up? You've seen my place so it's my turn to see yours. I'll bet you anything the décor is a reflection of the owner."

"You'll get to meet my roommate," Jana responded in the event Reese had any ideas he was going to finish what he started. "Winston is something of a character."

On the other end, Reese exhaled loudly. He regrouped and said, "You're living with a man and it's okay with him that you're going out with me? Is this what you call one of those open relationships?"

Jana chuckled. Reese sounded ticked.

"Winston and I are not involved," she corrected, cutting Reese a little slack. He didn't have to know that Winston might or might not be out of town. He just needed to be put on notice.

She'd missed her exit, dammit. All that going back and forth had her distracted. Better settle down.

"I'm on the road," Jana informed Reese. "I'll call with the address and directions to my place when I get home."

"Why didn't you say something before? We'll talk later, then. As for Sunday, I can't wait."

* * *

Reese hung up the phone thinking that he even liked the sound of Jana's voice. She always sounded breathless and a little husky. Her tone still held a bit of little-girl wonder to it.

He'd decided to make a quick call while he was seated in Bruce's waiting room waiting to see the developer. Reese had been surprised to be summoned to the sixth floor at the end of the day and hoped this wouldn't take long. He'd been looking forward to getting home and tackling one of the overgrown garden beds.

This would be the first time he'd seen Bruce since the incident out in front of the building. Over time he'd gotten used to being issued orders via the phone. There had been no further discussion about public spaces, so Reese had simply carried on with what he thought would work for the community and would in the long run be most beneficial.

Now he'd been sitting for what easily must be half an hour. He wondered whether Bruce had forgotten him. The secretary who'd been seated up front had packed up her belongings on the stroke of five and gone home. Could be she'd never told Bruce he was waiting.

Might as well find out if that was the case. Reese decided to go exploring. He'd stick his head into Bruce's office and remind him he was waiting. Maybe he'd even suggest they meet another time.

Reese started down the hallway, stopping to admire the black-and-white photos of projects in various stages of development. There were also some that had been successfully completed. The Rothschild organization had much to be proud of.

He stuck his head into several offices, amazed at the opulence in the office of those running the show.

There were sculptures and framed pieces of art that surely had cost a small fortune. The carpeting under-foot was cushy and didn't register footprints. Piped-in jazz music came from speakers up above. Even the floral arrangement on the assistant's desk, as well as those strategically placed in some of the other offices, didn't look like they were even a day old. Potted plants looked tended and well fed.

As he approached Bruce's office, Reese heard the sound of muted voices. To be expected, he supposed, since the man was seldom alone. He was about to apologize for interrupting when he heard what he thought might be Seth Bloom's voice say, "We should count our lucky stars the city manager is loyal."

"What does loyalty have to do with anything?" Bruce asked. "He owes us."

"Same thing, but at least he came through. If he hadn't acted, or rather not acted, the lease on Lake-view Park would have been renewed. We would never have gotten that property."

"I think we should be grateful the old coot who owns the property is damn near senile. Anyone else would have questioned the reason for the city not re-newing that lease."

"I suppose. The important thing is we got it for a steal," Seth piped in. "We shouldn't complain. We were handed a gift."

"I'm not complaining. Never complaining when I'm making money."

Reese cleared his throat, then stuck his head inside the doorway. He'd mull over later what he'd overheard.

"Sorry to interrupt," he said, glancing at his watch.

Both men jumped and looked like they could bene-fit from an antacid.

"You did say you wanted to see me," Reese reminded Bruce. "I thought you might have forgotten I was waiting."

"I did." Bruce answered, quickly gathering his composure and getting to his feet. "I was just going over a few things with Seth before we call it an evening. Can you hang in for a while? If not we can get together over breakfast first thing tomorrow. My personal trainer comes by at six, so seven thirty would work. We could meet in the executive cafeteria."

"Yes, tomorrow morning would be better for me. I'd like to get home and put a dent in my garden before it gets dark," Reese answered. "How are you, Seth?" He nodded at the man he was really beginning to dislike.

Seth Bloom didn't acknowledge his greeting—not surprising given their last encounter. Reese had often wondered what the true relationship was between the vice president of acquisitions and Bruce. At times it seemed that Seth was running the show, or attempting to run it. Now the man sat with his eyes narrowed, probably wondering just how much Reese had overheard. Well, let him wonder.

Something was definitely rotten in the city of San Diego. Reese could smell it. He would find out what was causing the stench if it took his last breath.

Seth and Bruce's conversation had confirmed exactly what he'd been thinking. Why, after all these years of leasing a property to the city, had the owner decided to sell? From everything he'd heard about Horace Lakatos, he didn't need the money.

Curiosity had prompted Reese to find out as much as he could about the Lakeview Park property owner. He'd discovered that Horace was from old money and prided himself on his benevolence. He owned several pieces of prime real estate, which he'd leased to the city as well as to private enterprise. He held the deed to acres and acres of land.

There should have been more of a flap made by the city council when Lakatos chose not to renew to the city. Someone should have contacted Horace to find out his reasoning. Then again maybe Horace was never contacted, which was why the lease was allowed to revert back to him. It seemed complicated and slimy but not impossible. It was definitely something to think about later.

Reese made a mental note to do a little digging. He knew just whom he would contact on the city council board. Yvonne would be happy to hear from him. He was not above taking advantage of her interest in him to get the information he needed. Heck, he might even invite her to lunch.

"Until tomorrow, then," Reese said, turning and leaving.

"Sure thing."

As Reese left he could feel Seth's eyes on his back. He would be a man to watch. They shared a mutual dislike.

"Do you think he overheard us?" Bruce asked Seth the moment he was sure Reese was out of earshot.

"I'm not sure."

"You don't like the designer, do you?"

"I don't trust the guy. I'm not sure he's on our side. I'm not sure he's hungry enough."

Bruce rolled a Waterman fountain pen back and forth between moist palms. "What's 'not hungry enough' supposed to mean?"

"It means that he doesn't need us. It's not wise having anyone on our team who isn't beholden. We've worked too long and hard to have anyone tip the applecart."

"Agreed."

Bruce stood. "I could use a drink. How about you?"

"Yeah, a couple would go down nicely. Ever thought of checking out Reese's credentials?"

Bruce shrugged. "Not sure I would find anything. He came highly recommended with degrees from some of the best schools. His advanced degrees are from the University of Miami and Harvard. You don't get better than that."

"He must have a skeleton or two in his closet," Seth said sagely. "Our job is to find bones we can rattle. We need that man in our pocket. He's a loose canon and arrogant to boot."

"Arrogant or stupid," Bruce said, gathering his suit jacket. "If he just does what I say, he'll have work for years."

"Why don't you just fire him?"

"And risk a lawsuit? He's doing his job. It's his allegiance I'm concerned about. Besides, it's too late to hire another designer. We're in too deep. I can't risk this project being held up further."

"Good point."

With that both men headed out.

Chapter 14

"You can't wear that old thing," Winston said, frowning. Placing a hand on his hip, he circled Jana. "That skirt's got to go. A little too retro."

"I am retro. I've always been retro."

"Not today, darling. You need to be happening. Boyfriend's got to take one look at you and want to jump your bones."

Jana groaned loudly. "Winston, aren't you going to be late for your flight?"

Winston picked up his wrist and squinted at his watch. "Nope. I have plenty of time. Let's see what you have in that closet."

He didn't wait to be granted permission. He simply marched into Jana's walk-in closet. It would be pointless to protest or insist he mind his own business, Winston would just ignore her.

The telephone rang and Jana went off to answer it.

"If it's crew scheduling, I'm not home," Winston called from the inner recesses. "I don't want anyone messing with my trip. I've got a hot date in Rome."

The moment Jana picked up the phone, Twyla started in.

"You're still home?"

"Why wouldn't I be?"

"Isn't today the day of your date?"

"Yes, the last time I checked. What is it you want, Twyla?"

"Oh, nothing."

Nothing her foot.

"Then in that case I have to go," Jana said, preparing to hang up.

"Wait. Wait. You will call me with all the details," Twyla pleaded.

What was it with everyone? They acted as if a date with Reese McDonald was like having an audience with the pope.

The phone rang again. Twyla again, most likely.

"What now?" Jana grumbled.

"Is that any way to greet your mother?"

Jana rolled her eyes. Dealing with Mona while she was trying to get ready for a date was the last thing she needed.

"Hello, Mother," Jana said dutifully.

"Is he there?"

"Is who here, Mother?"

"Reese. Now don't be coy, baby."

Jana expelled a long sigh, one she hoped her mother heard loud and clear. "Not yet, Mother. I was trying to get dressed."

"What are you wearing?"

Why was everyone so interested in her clothes? She thought she dressed smartly, with panache and style.

"I'm trying to decide."

"What about that lovely sundress from Neiman's?" Mona prodded.

"No, too fancy. I'm going to a street fair, Mother, not out for cocktails."

"Jana, love, I've found it," Winston called from the doorway.

"Gotta run, Mother. Love you."

Jana hung up while Mona was still carrying on about women needing to remember to be women. It was an age-old lecture and one Jana was tired of. Her mother grew up in an era when men still held doors open and carried women's packages. Mona would be horrified at the thought of splitting a check. She'd grown up at a time where women were coming into their own, but she'd missed the revolution as well as the entire women's movement. She'd been much too busy getting degrees.

Winston was tapping a navy Gucci loafer impatiently. During Jana's absence he'd put on his uniform. Now he was standing holding a skirt and camisole top she didn't remember she owned.

"Where did you find those?" Jana asked wrinkling her nose.

"In a paper bag in the back of your closet." He sniffed. "With tags from your favorite consignment shop. But at least the pieces are new. Someone had good taste."

Implying she didn't. The skirt Winston held out to her was sheer white chiffon and ruffled from waistband to hem. The top was a pretty turquoise with tiny spaghetti straps.

"Go on, try them," Winston urged, folding turquoise and silver earrings and a matching necklace he'd found, from God knew where, into her palms." He stood back assessing her and tapping an index finger against her cheek. "We've got to do something with that hair. The blonde is done. I mean passé."

Only a gay man would notice.

"I don't have time to worry about that," Jana said, grabbing the clothing Winston thrust at her. "The man's going to be here in less than an hour and you need to leave for your trip."

"Oh, I have plenty of time," Winston said, flopping down on the couch. "Boyfriend will need to pass my inspection, if you know what I mean. Despite what you hear, darling, size does matter. I intend to size him up and tell you if the package is worth it."

"Winston!" Jana cried, horrified.

In her bedroom, Jana slipped on the gauze skirt and pulled the camisole over her head. She vaguely remembered buying the clothes. It had been one of those rare days when she'd felt a bit down and needed a pick-me-up. She'd bought on impulse and then promptly forgotten why she'd done so.

Hurrying now, Jana popped on the earrings and matching necklace. Perfect! Winston's taste as always was impeccable. Much as he annoyed her at times, she'd come to rely on his honesty and sharp tongue. He'd kept her from making mistakes both professionally and personally.

"Are you decent, Jana dear?" Winston called from the outer room.

It wouldn't have mattered if she were butt naked. She was not what Winston was looking for.

"I'm dressed," Jana called back.

"Good!"

Winston came flouncing in carrying a straw hat. "This should pull the whole thing together and hide the hair that makes you look like a scarecrow." He plopped the hat on Jana's head and pursed his lips. "Now let me think."

Jana didn't even want to know where Winston had come up with the hat. It looked like something one of his friends might have left behind. Or maybe he'd bought it for himself on a whim.

He crossed over to the dresser Jana had refinished in bright coats of pink-and-yellow lacquer, and began searching through her stacked hatboxes. "Got it!" Winston said, holding up a broach with two irises in full bloom. "Pop this right on the front of that hat and you'll be happening."

The straw hat was then unceremoniously taken off her head and the pin attached. Winston then sniffed as if he smelled something unpleasant. "What fragrance are you wearing?"

"Eau de Nothing."

"That's what I thought."

Jana had had enough. She'd allowed him to dress her but that's where it ended. Winston was not picking out perfume for her. The choice of a fragrance would be hers and hers alone. If she went au naturale, then that was her choice.

The buzzer went off. Horrified, Jana glanced at the watch on her ring.

"He's here? What do I say? Do?"

"Work it, girlfriend," Winston answered, swaggering off to answer.

"Winston, please don't embarrass me!"

He didn't answer.

Jana took a deep breath and willed her heart to stop racing. She hadn't seen Reese since . . . Well, since he'd kissed her, and they'd come damn close to landing in bed. Better get out there before Winston said something or acted in some inappropriate way and sent the man running.

Jana raced out of the bedroom just as Winston yanked the door open.

"Are those for me?" Jana heard him ask. He was flirting shamelessly.

"Only if you're the mistress of the house," Reese's equally smooth reply came.

Winston's laughter came in ripples. He moved aside to let Reese enter. "You're okay, boyfriend. You can hold your own. Jana," he screamed at the top of his lungs.

"I'm here right behind you," Jana said more quietly. "Reese, it's nice to see you again."

Winston was gathering the rollerboard he kept parked in the living room. He picked up his tote bag. "Well, I'm off, you two have fun now. And Jana about the size of that package we were discussing—"

"Have a safe trip, Winston," Jana hissed, her hand on the small of his back, easing him out. "Thanks for the help."

"Don't mention it."

At last they were alone. Reese was still standing there holding a smartly wrapped combination of irises, honeysuckle, roses, and ferns. The combination smelled heavenly.

"For you," he said, thrusting the arrangement at her. "From my garden."

Jana accepted the bouquet and sniffed at it appreciatively. "They're lovely. Thank you."

"You're lovely," he answered. "A gift, and what a hard-working designer deserves after a hellish week."

Jana thanked him again and totally flustered, raced off to the kitchen where she found a vase and quickly began arranging his flowers. She returned to place them on the coffee table she'd made, using two ceramic urns and the glass a neighbor had thrown out in the trash.

"Ready?" she asked Reese.

"I am if you are."

They took his Range Rover, Jana playing navigator as they drove the short distance to La Mesa where the annual Art and Jazz Festival was held on the boulevard.

"Are we almost there?" Reese asked. "You did say it was only about a ten-mile drive."

"And we've only been driving fifteen minutes. Next exit." Jana pointed to a sign announcing the picturesque village.

Reese followed her directions and got off. They headed for La Mesa Boulevard, which was the main thoroughfare and home to dozens of mom-and-pop businesses.

La Mesa was a quaint community with a population of a little under sixty thousand. It had kept its small-town feel. The older part of the city had streets lined with antique shops and quaint little eateries. And like most older Southern California communities, it drew an eclectic group of residents, many of them artists and musicians.

"See those hills over there?" Jana said pointing to the surrounding hillside. "There are a gazillion ranch-style homes nestled in them old hills. Families with kids move to this area because of its good schools and low crime rate."

Reese listened while looking for a place to park. He nodded his head and kept circling blocks. Half of San Diego seemed to be here for the festival.

"Might as well follow the signs for festival parking," Jana suggested, "long as those lines are."

They inched their way toward what must have been an abandoned lot now reserved for parking. "So is this where you grew up?" Reese asked.

"No, I grew up in La Jolla."

It suddenly struck her they knew very little about each other's backgrounds.

Her response produced the usual reaction. Reese's sherry gaze met hers head-on. "That's a pretty affluent area."

She heard what he was not saying. "It is."

"Well, you can't just leave me hanging. Sounds like your family wasn't hurting. Fill me in."

What did he care?

"Both of my parents are doctors," Jana reluctantly admitted.

"That's impressive. Needless to say they instilled their work ethic in their daughter." Reese took one hand off the steering wheel and squeezed her hand. "That's a compliment by the way."

Jana had never thought of herself as being particularly driven. She believed in balance. Work hard. Play hard. And she'd been considered to be something of a free spirit most of her life. At one point she'd even thought she might be adopted. She and her parents were as different as people could be. Even their values were different. They cared about material things. She cared about people. No, perhaps she wasn't being fair, they must care about people, or they would never have chosen the professions they were in. Frankly she just didn't understand them.

Mona remained mired in tradition. She cared what people thought. She'd never been able to understand her Bohemian daughter. And Gordon, still smitten by his wife of almost thirty years, claimed he found joy in delivering his babies. And so he spent more time at the hospital than at home; that didn't make a whole lot of sense.

What it boiled down to was the almighty dollar. She'd benefited from her parents' money when she was growing up. But what she'd really needed most was them—not some fancy toy. Jana would have gladly traded everything she owned for their undivided attention. Having both parents at her dance recitals or softball games would have been a dream come true.

It was Carmen, the housekeeper, who took Jana to her recitals. It was Carmen who picked her up from the softball games. Carmen had been her surrogate mother. Always Carmen.

And so she'd chosen social work, low paying but rewarding. It grounded her in reality and reminded her of how fortunate she was. By the grace of God, she was not one of her clients. Her job filled a void. The role fulfilled her need to be needed and gave her a family.

"I've met your mother. She's elegant, well spoken, and quite smart," Reese said, interrupting her thoughts as he aimed the nose of the vehicle into a spot the attendant pointed out. "What's your father like?"

"He's a father."

This would be a telling moment. Jana seldom mentioned that her father was white. She found it irrelevant. He was her dad, plain and simple. His pigmentation was no one's business and shouldn't matter.

"I guess I've been put in my place."

She didn't answer him.

Reese came to the passenger side and opened the door. Still deep in thought, Jana allowed him to help her out. He paid the attendant and they began walking toward the boulevard.

She'd grown up as the offspring of parents of different ethnicities. It had allowed her to see the ugly side of people as well as the deep humanity that the most unexpected people showed. She'd pretty much seen and heard it all.

Jana loved being the product of blended cultures. Her grandparents on her father's side were liberals who'd embraced Mona into the family. They'd teased Gordon mercilessly about being fortunate enough to find a woman who would put up with him. And they adored Jana.

Jana's maternal grandparents had been active in the Civil Rights movement. They'd grown up at a time when blacks were forced to use different restrooms from whites and give up their seats on buses. Yet they'd maintained enormous pride and a calm dignity. They saw the good in all people. Jana had learned from them to be proud of who she was, and to stand firm in her beliefs. They'd made her listen to the greats: Ella, Sarah, The Duke, and The Count. That's where her appreciation for good jazz and big band music had come.

"Am I boring you?" Reese joked, again breaking into her thoughts. "Maybe your parents aren't together and I've overstepped my bounds."

Jana turned her smile on him. "Oh, they're very together. Dad's an obstetrician and still quite busy. He worships the ground my mother walks on."

"I admire a brother, especially of his generation, who's not afraid to show how he feels about his lady."

She'd been given the perfect opening. Who cared how Reese reacted? It would tell her something about him.

"My father's not a brother," she said. "Although he would like to think of himself as such."

A beat or two went by, maybe three. "That explains the locks," Reese said, fingering what he could of the curls that peeked out from under her hat.

He'd risen another notch in her estimation for taking it all in stride. Jana playfully smacked his hand away. "No it doesn't, it's dyed. I chose the color because it complements my complexion and because I like it."

"What's not to like?"

Jana beamed at him, forgetting momentarily that she was still upset because he'd taken a passive role in a situation that mattered to her very much.

They were now approaching an area on the boulevard with tents. Many dogs were being walked on leashes, and the smallest ones carried clutch-style.

"What's your father like?" Jana asked as they stopped in front of a tent selling soy candles. She picked up a container and sniffed one.

"Dead," Reese said.

That single word got her attention. Jana placed a hand on his arm. "Now am I being insensitive? I'm so sorry."

"Nothing to be sorry about. My father was a good man and well intentioned. He just didn't quite know what to do with my brother, Barry, and me."

"And your mother?"

The vendor was now wending his way over to them.

"Just browsing," Jana quickly said, taking Reese's hand and moving him away.

"Sure you don't want a candle? I'll buy it for you," Reese offered.

It was sweet of him but she didn't need a candle.

She had more than her share back at the apartment. Jana loved the delicious smells and the calming effect of the various scents. Winston bought one in every place he visited. There wasn't a shape, size, or fragrance they didn't have.

They continued up the street and Jana continued to probe. "I was asking about your mother. Was she the kind of mom every child dreams of? You know—warm, cuddly, and sweet, accepting that you weren't going to be perfect?"

They were still holding hands. "I wouldn't know," he said. "I have no memory of her."

"Oh, Reese, I really am batting a hundred today. I'm sorry. She died too, that must have been tough."

"No, she ran off with the next-door neighbor." Reese said it nonchalantly as if it didn't hurt. "Broke my old man's heart. I don't think he ever recovered."

"And broke yours too."

"Can we talk about something else?"

"Sure."

They continued walking and talking about whatever struck their fancy, anything but family. Jana was enjoying it all. The perfect California day, the browsing, and the company of a man whom at first she'd disliked.

At the end of the first row of tents, vendors with kiosks were peddling their food.

"How about a veggie wrap?" Reese suggested.

He was attentive and considerate. He'd remembered she didn't eat meat. Little things like that mattered.

Wrap in hand they continued on their way. Then Reese surprised her by saying, "I'd like to buy you a gift. And I know exactly what you'd like."

"You do?"

He tugged on her hand, propelling her toward one of the tents they'd gone into before.

She let him. Reese McDonald was turning out to be sweet.

Chapter 15

"Oh, Reese, I can't let you spend that much money on me," Jana cried.

"We'll take it," Reese said to the artist who stood with paper and ribbon in hand looking from one to the other.

"Oh no we won't."

They bickered back and forth for a good five minutes. Reese had wanted to buy Jana the gift from the moment he'd seen how her eyes lit up when she'd spotted the painting. He'd never been the type of man to try to buy a woman. But this was one woman he wanted to impress.

The portrait was perfect. While it wasn't a personal gift like a piece of jewelry it would be memorable in its own way. An African American woman sat on a dock, her bare feet dangling inches over the blue Pacific Ocean. Her head was tilted to the side, gazing at the azure sky. Her smile was dreamy and there was a faraway look in her eyes. Her expression reminded Reese of Jana's when she thought no one was looking.

They continued to argue over the cost, going back and forth and back again.

"So what will it be?" the artist asked, finally growing impatient. Several potential customers had come by and moved on. Reese was well aware they'd taken up enough of the man's time.

"We'll take it," Reese said, gesturing to the artist to wrap up the portrait.

"We will not," Jana insisted, hissing under her breath. "I can't allow you to spend one hundred and fifty dollars on me. We barely know each other."

"It's only money." He plopped his American Express card into the open palm of the vendor. "Wrap it up and put one of those pretty turquoise ribbons on it."

Jana huffed out a breath and tapped a sandaled foot, signaling her irritation with him. "Whatever. But I don't like accepting gifts from men."

"Then pretend I'm a woman."

His comment produced another huffed breath.

The vendor's lips twitched but he made quick work of bundling the artwork and adding a festive ribbon.

"There you go," the artist said handing it over to Jana. "Enjoy. You've got a quality man. Make sure you take good care of him."

"He's not . . ."

"Darling, we have to go," Reese, said kissing the top of her hat and steering her through the open flap of the tent.

"What was that all about?" Jana asked when they were on the crowded sidewalk again. "We're hardly at the 'darling' stage. Besides, I'm not particularly happy with you."

"And why is that?"

"We'll talk about it on the drive back."

"Okay."

Reese began to steer her back the way they'd come.

"Are we leaving, then?" Jana asked, puzzled.

She probably figured they'd be exploring the charming little village on foot. They'd been at the festival only a couple of hours. The truth is he'd planned on just that.

"Yup."

"Why?"

"Make up your mind, darling. Either you're mad at me or you're not."

"Are you always like this?" Jana asked, setting down her gift on the sidewalk and throwing her arms in the air.

"Like what?"

"Infuriating. Impossible to reason with."

He continued to walk. "So reason with me," he said over his shoulder. "What have I done to upset you?"

"You know damn well what you've done."

Jana came to a full stop in the center of the charming bridge they were crossing. It spanned a man-made waterway, and the peak of Mount Helix east of La Mesa could clearly be seen.

"It's a disgrace the way that Lottie Addison and Hugh Pilgrim were treated," she said.

He had a faint idea what she was talking about but couldn't be sure. "Sorry, am I supposed to know who these people are?"

"They're elderly and infirm, and that horrible man you work for had them arrested. Those two old people spent the night in jail."

"I'm sorry. Truly sorry it happened," he said. He could tell she was really worked up. "Things got out of hand I heard. If I were running the show I would have handled things very differently."

Jana's eyes were now steel gray.

"I thought you *were* running the show."

Reese realized there would be no reasoning with her this afternoon. "Okay, on behalf of the Rothschilds I apologize."

That incensed her even further. Jana stamped her foot. "That's not good enough. What's to become of these folks? Where are they to go for recreation and food? What about those options you discussed? What's their status?"

"I'm working on it," Reese said, attempting to take her hand again.

Jana pulled out of his reach. "Not good enough."

Reese shot her what he hoped was a pleading look. "All I need to do is book time with Bruce and discuss the revised plans with him."

She looked at him suspiciously, as if not sure whether to believe him or not. "What's the real problem?" Jana asked more calmly. "We're talking forty acres. Why can't even a half an acre be dedicated to making the community happy?"

"I was thinking more along the lines of three."

That got her attention. "Please," she pleaded, "can't you try harder to make that happen? It would go a long way to repairing the damage already done."

He would if he could. But first he needed to find out what had really happened with that lease. He'd put off calling Yvonne long enough. He'd remedy that as soon as he could.

"Am I forgiven, then?" Reese asked, reaching for Jana's hand. "Can we agree I'm not the enemy?"

"I suppose."

* * *

Two hours later they were back in her apartment. Reese had insisted on treating Jana to an early dinner, and despite her initial reservations, she found that she was enjoying his company immensely. It had become awkward only after he'd driven her back to the apartment and parked the car. She'd then felt obligated to ask him in.

Jana lost the straw hat while Reese examined every inch of living space. He lined up the old paperweights she collected in groupings of size and color.

"Are you always this organized?" Jana asked.

"Order is very important to me."

"Why?"

Jana recalled the trophies she'd seen at his home all meticulously lined up. She noted the conservative clothing that he seemed to favor, and even the contained manner in which he argued his point. The man needed to shake up a bit.

"You didn't answer," she teased.

He joined her on the couch where they'd both been sipping tea. "Because when you grow up in a world of disorder, order is very important to you."

"Then we definitely won't make good life partners," she joked, and could have bitten her tongue the moment it came out. "I'm the type of person who throws my clothing on chairs." She swept her hand in the direction of the dining area. "I keep my bills in piles on the table and pay them when I remember. I make up my bed once a week when I change the linens."

"How come?"

"How come what?" That was who she was, always had been.

"You're not more structured. Didn't you tell me

both of your parents were doctors? Some level of meticulousness must come with that territory."

"That, my friend, is exactly the point. You grow up in a house where everything has to be perfect. There's even a structure to how meals are cooked. You know you'll have steak on Sunday and baked salmon on Wednesday. There's a bulletin board in the kitchen where you leave and receive messages so that everyone knows your whereabouts. You spill juice on the carpeting by accident and my goodness you're made to feel as if you've committed a crime. The poor housekeeper, arthritic or not, is on her hands and knees with soda water getting the stain out. It's enough to drive a person crazy.

"Got it!" Reese said. "I would have killed for that kind of order when I was growing up. I must have spent most of my young life wearing mismatched socks because no one ever sorted and folded laundry in our house. You retrieved what you could from the hamper, clean and dirty clothing were stuffed in together."

He eased off the couch and stretched. "Where are you thinking of putting that portrait of yours?"

"In the bedroom."

Again she could kick herself. She really needed to start thinking before opening her big, fat mouth.

"I'll help you find a spot," Reese said, offering her a hand to help her up.

"Uh, that's not a good idea."

Reese hiked an eyebrow. "What are you afraid of?"

"I'm not afraid." But she was. She was afraid of him. The other eyebrow shot up. He was on to her.

"We're alone in your apartment anyway," he said. "Anything that could happen in your bedroom could happen right here." Reese pointed a finger. "On that very comfortable sofa."

She was not the type who blushed, yet she felt the warmth in her cheeks and the roar of blood in her ears. Reese had the uncanny ability to read her thoughts. That she found most unsettling. And yes, they'd been X-rated of late ever since she'd met him. She'd taken one glimpse of that fine, half-dressed body when they'd gone running, and all she'd been thinking of since was what Reese would look like naked.

"Do you have a hammer?" he asked. "And nails, little ones?"

"Somewhere."

Still flustered, Jana headed for the kitchen and the drawer where Winston kept his toolbox. She returned to the living room and handed it to Reese.

He followed her into her bedroom, pausing on the threshold to mutter, "You weren't kidding when you said you weren't exactly the most orderly person."

Jana had picked up the living room in preparation of Reese's visit. She'd stuffed magazines and newspapers, nail polish, and lotions into bags and tossed them on her unmade bed. Last week's clothing was still heaped on the chair waiting to be either hung or laundered. On the floor were towels and half a dozen pairs of shoes she'd stepped out of.

Jana made a wry face. He'd get over it.

"Sorry if I've offended your sensibilities," she said, gesturing toward all the empty wall space. "You choose. If need be we can move a couple of things around."

"Maybe that wall where you have those Mardi Gras masks." He stepped gingerly around the mess on the floor.

Jana approached the wall she'd painted Chinese red, holding her precious collection: the masks she'd collected from the various carnivals she'd attended in

New Orleans, Rio de Janeiro, and the Caribbean island of St. Vincent. She removed a sequined mask and held it up to her face.

"Maybe my friends will allow me to share the wall," she said in an exaggerated accent, peering through the eye slits at him.

"They should," he said, assuming a spooky voice and joining in the fun. "Me say they have vision and great taste."

Jana cracked up. That was another thing she liked about Reese. He got her crazy sense of humor and could loosen up when the time called for it.

Stepping over the towels and hastily discarded shoes, he joined her. As if totally captivated by the items adorning the wall, Reese said, sounding awed, "You really are an interesting woman. You don't give a damn what anyone thinks and you're not about pretensions. I like that a lot."

He was next to her now, much too close for comfort. He was making her feel like a nervous fifteen-year-old whose limbs had grown faster than her emotional development. She was starting to like the man, idiosyncrasies and all.

"I have another thought. Maybe the bathroom will work," Jana suggested, taking a step back and placing herself safely out of the way. The portrait might be more in keeping with the room's laid-back décor.

Reese followed her into the master bathroom. It was huge, more the size of a powder room in an upscale restaurant than what the standard apartment complex usually had to offer. When she'd first seen the room she'd envisioned herself languishing for hours in the huge step-down shower and Jacuzzi tub. Its potential had been the dealmaker.

The minute the ink was dry on Jana's lease she'd moved in. The first thing she'd done was to paint the walls a vivid sky blue. Then she'd gone out and purchased wicker furniture from the second-hand place down the street, and spent the next few weeks upholstering the divan and matching chair in a yellow-and-blue fabric that reminded her of days at the beach. Then Winston had come along, and even though it wasn't his bathroom, he'd added his touches: bamboo shades and a big fabric umbrella that hung upside down from the ceiling.

"Uhhhh," Reese said from the doorway, his eyebrows winged.

Jana saw him looking at the damp towels on the tile floor she'd left after taking her shower, the toiletries she'd been using still spilled across the counter top. He'd just have to get over it.

"Plenty of wall space in here," he acknowledged, sidestepping the towels. "But not a good place to hang a watercolor. Too damp."

Back they went to the bedroom.

Reese positioned the framed portrait against the wall next to a sequined-and-feathered mask.

"What do you think?" he asked.

"Hate it."

He pointed to a wall where a mirror hung. "Move that to here and it might work."

Jana stood watching as Reese hung the photo and pronounced its new location perfect. He made sure it wasn't lopsided and came back to wind one arm around her neck and the other around her waist. Reese stared at her for what seemed an eternity.

"Beautiful," he said, twirling a loose curl of her hair around his finger. "Simply beautiful." Glancing at the photo he'd just hung, and then back at her, he said, "She's not fit to walk in your shoes."

Jana liked the feeling of Reese's hands on her flesh. She pressed herself against his chest and let his arms encircle her. His body felt solid, familiar, and comfortable. Comfort was important to a woman who'd long ago decided to be true to herself.

A slight shift of her head and Reese was kissing her. Soon she was kissing him back and with a passion she didn't know she possessed. When his tongue swept her mouth she captured it, and when his hands crept under her camisole to knead the skin on her stomach, she made low, moaning sounds.

It was Jana who led Reese to her bed. It was she who, fully clothed, straddled him and began working free the buttons of his shirt. It was she who splayed her hand across his hairy chest, outlined his pectorals, and moved downward to make feathery circles on his ribs. She didn't seem to be able to get enough of him.

Reese's masculine scent filled her nostrils. The warmth of his flesh under her hand pulled her in. She wanted to be an extension of him, to feel every sinew and muscle of a body that was damn close to perfect. She wanted to dance that age-old dance that had started with Eve.

Reese must be a mind reader. He was already tugging off his shirt. Jana quickly lost her camisole and laid back, gloriously free, her breasts spilling. She'd once been told she had perfectly symmetrical breasts. Now her fingers worked a nipple, taunting him, teasing him, goading him to touch her in all the places that ached and pulsated.

Reese's lips were on her breasts, tugging gently. He laved her nipples until they pebbled. His hand slid between the elastic waistband of her skirt, fingers stroking her heated skin and plucking at the thong panties that made her feel sexy and womanly.

Jana ran an open palm across his burgeoning erection. "Nice."

Reese covered her hand, pressing her palm against the length of him. Even through the expensive fabric of his trousers she could feel him pulsating. Jana slid his zipper down, reached in and around his Michael Jordan shorts and set him free.

He sprang to life in her hands.

"Oh my."

Reese's swollen member stood at full attention now. Jana took him into her hands stroking, teasing, squeezing. The pad of her thumb outlined the seam that ran the length of him, and then her fingers gently cupped his scrotum.

Reese groaned and gyrated under her ministrations. He was going to be a whole lot more vocal by the time she was through.

"Take off your clothes, baby," Reese said, his excited breathing coming in short spurts as if he'd just run a mile. Sitting up, he quickly removed his pants and folded them. That act brought a smile to Jana's face.

He reached into his back pocket, removed his wallet, and found a foil package. He tossed the wallet on an African drum that served as her night table. "We'll need this," he said, "pays to be safe."

"Pays to be smart," Jana quipped. Oh, what the heck, she liked the man. Actually, more than liked him, and she wasn't some insecure teenager, like Lucy, who would be brokenhearted if nothing further came of it. Not every union had to lead to something. It had been a while since she'd made love to anyone and she sensed making love to Reese would be good—no, better than good.

Jana ditched her skirt and carefully removed the thong that was her one modern clothing indulgence. In her opinion it was the greatest invention man ever made. She loved the way the silk felt against her skin and how the material settled high on her hips, leaving her buttocks free and exposed. Wearing it made her feel powerful and sexy, and she didn't have to worry about panty lines.

"Look at you," Reese growled, standing to slip out of the thigh-hugging undershorts encasing his muscular legs. He stood in all his male glory: erect, ready, and able. Jana plopped back down on the bed.

Reese kneeled next to her. His fingers dipped into the tight curls at her apex. He used his fingers to confirm she was moist and ready to move on to the next stage of their lovemaking.

Head bowed he slowly went to work on her until she was a gasping, whimpering mass of need. Jana came damn close to bouncing off the ceiling. When the first wave of ecstasy hit her she bit her bottom lip. But Reese was relentless, he would not let up. Holding her close he got back to business.

Jana rode the second wave, locking her legs around his neck and pressing into him. She was long past restraint and was fully enjoying every glorious moment.

Tears spilled down her cheeks as her body arched and bucked. Jana's body spasmed. She cried out. Then there was sweet release.

It was Reese's turn. Now she would be merciless.

She was on her knees taking him into her mouth, twining her fingers around his, and burying herself in the scent of him.

When he groaned she turned up the heat a notch, picking up the rhythm. Reese's fingers were in her hair. He tugged gently—his signal he wanted to change positions.

He shifted onto his back, and slipped on the condom before curving a finger at her.

"Come here, babe."

Jana lowered herself onto him until she was impaled. Her ankles cushioned his solid hips and his warmth filled her insides. Reese eased onto his elbows and began pumping, intensifying his thrusts with each new entry.

Jana was flying high. She squeezed, released, and squeezed again, using every muscle she had to trap and hold him. He let out one long, agonizing groan, and she came with him.

She could smell him, feel him, hear him.

A ridiculous thought surfaced: what would it be like to have this man's baby?

She'd gotten ahead of herself. This was a hook up. A one-time thing. No guarantee it would ever be repeated, even if she wanted it.

Chapter 16

Reese felt ridiculously guilty as he waited for Yvonne Munoz to show up. He'd lured the woman to the restaurant under false pretenses, he supposed. Yvonne probably thought it was a date.

She had been so excited when he'd called. And although he did not want to mislead her, what he really needed was vital information. He didn't know anyone on the city council other than her.

Guilt made him ask the maître d' of the chichi restaurant to get him a good table. And she'd come through, seating him at what she called one of her primo tables: a spot to see and be seen. But dammit he didn't necessarily want to be seen with Yvonne, it was Jana he wanted. Now where did that come from?

Yvonne, helmet-hair and all, breezed in, scanning the room. The maître d' was at her side almost immediately, guiding her toward the table where he waited.

"Thank you," Yvonne said, passing on the chair the woman held out, and sliding into one next to Reese.

Her stockinged thigh grazed the material of his

slacks. This was not starting off well. Reese moved his leg out of the way.

"Sorry," Yvonne said, throwing him what she thought was a sexy smile.

Reese decided he liked his women a heck of a lot more subtle and not as ready to pounce as this one was. He liked women who were looser and not filled with pretensions, women extremely comfortable with themselves who didn't make excuses for having flaws.

Jana's beautiful face filled his vision again. The intensity and intimacy of their lovemaking had given him reason for reflection. And although he hadn't gotten around to calling her yet, he couldn't get her out of his mind.

"How have you been?" Reese asked Yvonne as the waiter poured water into their glasses.

"Busy. There's a lot happening with the city these days. It's always one meeting or another."

She'd given him the perfect opening. He wouldn't have to waste time with half an hour of small talk. "Speaking of which. What's happening with Lakeview's permits?"

Yvonne took a slow sip of water. "Is that why you invited me to lunch? And to think I was hoping you were interested in me as a woman." Another sly smile followed.

"I'm interested in you as a person," Reese said, skillfully sidestepping the question.

Yvonne blinked behind her glasses. "Then how come you haven't returned my phone calls? I've left you at least three messages."

"Busy, I guess. Sorry."

Reese decided he'd have to try another tact and get them back on track.

"I've never had the pleasure of meeting your city manager. What's he like?" he asked.

"You mean Carlos Pinellas?"

Menus were now being handed to them. Yvonne took her time perusing the choices before setting her menu aside.

"If you'd like to meet him in person, you can tomorrow evening. There's a ribbon-cutting ceremony in Hillcrest followed by cocktails. I need an escort." She arched her eyebrows suggestively. No mistaking the hint.

And while Reese didn't want to be further involved with the woman, it was too good an opportunity to pass up.

"I might be persuaded to escort you," he said. "What's this in honor of?"

"Our new performance center. It's been a long time in coming. There should be quite the turnout. The attire is semiformal. You'll pick me up, then?"

"Of course."

Their waiter returned ready to take their order. Reese, without even glancing at the menu, already knew what he was having. No heavy meals for him at this time of day. He'd heard the poached salmon here was wonderful. Gentleman that he was, he let Yvonne place her order first.

Throughout the meal they talked about one thing or another, but even so Reese was bored. Yvonne was one of those stiffly articulate people, politically correct to a fault, who parroted other people's opinions and didn't seem to have a personality of her own.

He was almost relieved when a woman's voice came out of the blue.

"Reese, is that you?"

He turned and squinted in the direction of a dark-skinned woman with close-cropped hair. She looked familiar but he couldn't place her. Then it came to him. She was Jana's business partner and friend.

Busted. Well, not exactly. There was no reason to feel guilty. He and Jana didn't have an understanding. They were having fun. Exploring. Getting to know each other.

"Twyla Lewis," Jana's friend reminded him, sticking out her hand. She flashed a smile in the direction of Yvonne. "Aren't you Councilwoman Munoz?"

Yvonne's wintry smile acknowledged the comment. "I am. Have we met?"

"Yes, as a matter of fact we have." Twyla was practically bubbling over and even seemed a bit awed by the city councilwoman. Reese sensed it was all an act.

"You may not remember me," Twyla said, "but I catered and planned an event in Pacific Beach a few weeks ago, the one you attended with Reese. You were also at the charity brunch my partner, Jana and I planned, the one for Professional Women in San Diego. It was a charity auction."

Yvonne squinted at Twyla as if trying to recall. "Ah, yes, I do remember you. It was your partner's mother who out-bid me for Reese." She chuckled as if it was the most ridiculous thing.

Twlya, to her credit, maintained her bubbly disposition.

"Jana and Reese are actually very well suited," she said. "They balance each other out perfectly. I'm sure Reese told you their date went well. I even heard something about seeing each other regularly. So, safe to say, Dr. Davis's money was well spent."

Score one for Twyla. She was no shrinking violet.

Yvonne looked like someone had taken an ice pick to her heart.

Reese decided to step in before the conversation got way out of hand.

"So what brings you here, Twyla?"

"Oh, the people I work with go out on Fridays." Twyla waved in the direction of a crowded table, then went on to explain. "We choose a different restaurant each time."

"The prelude to a relaxing weekend, then," Reese added.

"Exactly. Look, I've taken up enough of your time. Let me get back to the group. See you around."

Nodding in the councilwoman's direction, Twyla departed.

It looked as if the breadsticks Yvonne had been snapping and popping into her mouth—as a substitute for Twyla's head—had not settled well.

Fortunately, the waiter chose that moment to return with their order and the awkward moment passed. They moved on to speak of the Lakeview development and tomorrow's social event.

Reese couldn't wait to meet Carlos Pinellas.

Twyla could hardly contain herself. The moment she arrived back on the job she was on the phone to Jana.

"I've got exactly five minutes between counseling sessions," Jana said, sounding rushed. "So better say what you're going to say quickly."

"I'm just back from lunch with the gang at Mercy." Twyla stretched out the moment.

"Sounds like fun," Jana said dutifully. "You do this every Friday."

"Yes. But it's not every Friday that I run into Reese McDonald."

"Yeah?"

Twyla could hear the caution in her friend's voice.

"Your honey was having lunch with Yvonne Munoz."

Twyla waited through the audible exhaling of a long, drawn-out breath.

"Reese McDonald is not my honey," came Jana's predictable answer.

"Okay, so he's not. Let me rephrase it. Last week's date was lunching with Councilwoman Munoz."

"It was probably business."

"Monkey business."

Twyla sensed her friend's hurt. She hadn't meant to be the one to tell Jana but what were friends for? Jana needed to know what she was up against if she became further involved with the urban designer.

"Yvonne seemed rather proprietary," Twyla added.

"Perhaps she has reason to be."

"You're upset," Twyla confirmed. "Maybe I shouldn't have told you."

"Don't be silly. I have no claim on Reese."

But Twyla could tell from Jana's clipped tone that a change of subject might be in order. "How's Lucy doing?" she asked.

"Much better since she's dating Roberto. And of course since she's lost interest in Drew he's begun to pay her attention again. Hopefully she's smart enough to figure out what's up."

"Boy's up for a booty call."

"You got it."

"Speaking of which, has Reese called you?" Twyla asked, her curiosity needing to be satisfied.

"No, he has not called."

Twyla heard the hurt in her friend's voice.

Twyla persisted. "Will you be calling him?"

"Doubtful."

"Why not?

"We're at a standoff."

"Impasse, I call it."

"Same thing," Jana said. "I really have to go. Touch base later?"

"Sure."

Jana was still mildly irritated when her next appointment arrived. She left the mother of five seated outside in the waiting area and took a few minutes to regroup. Why did she feel she'd been used? Because after you had wonderful sex with a man you expected a call, that's why. And so far that phone call had not happened.

But maybe that was all it was about, just wonderful sex. It was foolish of her to expect more. Even so, she'd kept a constant ear out for the phone. It was the anticipation of Reese's call that had her on pins and needles. It was the sound of his voice that made her adrenaline flow. And here he was out at some fancy restaurant yakking it up with the Munoz woman.

What a fool she had been.

"Linda, I'm sorry," Jana said, entering the waiting room the social workers referred to as the "holding pen."

Linda—a buxom, overweight woman with a bright smile—rose, acknowledging the greeting. Her clothing, although inexpensive, was clean and meticulously pressed.

"Please follow me," Jana said, leading the way back to her office.

For the next half an hour Jana listened intently. But as the session wound down her attention wandered. She'd thought a second date with Reese was a sure thing but the longer he remained silent the more it seemed unlikely to happen.

What if, as Twyla suggested, she called Reese? Twenty-first-century women didn't have to wait for the man to call. Women asked men out all the time. She could take the ball and run with it. She'd ask him out for the next date. After all, she wanted to see him again.

Decision made, Jana refocused and gave Linda her undivided attention. The counseling session ended on an uplifting note and, as was her habit, Jana hugged her client and sent her off with a kiss.

During the session, Jana had come up with a plan. She wasn't just going to lie down, roll over, and let Yvonne Munoz walk off with Reese. Councilwoman Munoz needed to know there was competition, and stiff competition at that.

Jana Davis was no one's pushover.

Reese was naked to the waist and stripping the wooden floors of the rented house when the cell phone, tucked in his pocket, vibrated. Setting aside the machine he was using, he fumbled to find the instrument. Of course by then the phone had stopped ringing. He squinted at the missed number, recognizing it as vaguely familiar.

He crossed over to the kitchen and poured himself a glass of water. When the message light on the phone popped up he depressed the buttons to retrieve his message. Jana's voice made him smile. Even the cadence of her words filled him with energy. He compared her to salsa: hot, tangy, and exciting.

Not wanting to miss a word, Reese replayed the message several times. Jana was going on about a charity run that would benefit babies with the HIV virus. She wanted him to call her back if he was interested in join-ing her. Following the run there would be a beach party she wanted to attend.

Just hearing Jana's voice made him feel like he could take on the world. Reese took another long swal-low of water and rested his butt against the kitchen counter. He hit the RETURN CALL button, and waited.

"Hello, this is Jana."

"This is Reese."

His pulse for some unknown reason was throbbing like crazy.

"Yes, I know," she laughingly said.

Caller ID was sometimes not a beautiful thing.

"I'm calling to accept your invitation. The charity run seems to be for a good cause and the beach party sounds fun and exciting. Give me the details."

Jana rattled off the time and day and told him where the runners were scheduled to meet. "How are the plans coming along for Lakeview Park?" she asked. "Anything new?"

Always the damn park, they never seemed to be able to get away from that topic. There were times Reese wondered whether Jana was really interested in him or only in what she thought he might be able to do for the community and these people she'd bonded with. But wisely, he kept his own counsel.

"The group's starting to get antsy again," Jana said. "This time the talk is about a full-fledged demonstra-tion in front of the park. Things are liable to get ugly."

"Bruce is stalling," Reese admitted. "I can't pin him down. He keeps waffling back and forth. I've been try-ing to get in and speak with him so he has a clear un-derstanding of what I'm doing. So far no luck."

Jana made an exasperated sound. "This has to affect

the date of the groundbreaking," she said. "With what's going on, the date is probably going to get pushed back."

"The holdup has to do with permits. If they don't come through soon, we'll be screwed."

"I'll try to pacify the group," Jana offered in a surprising turn of events. "Maybe I can get them to exercise a bit of patience. I may be able to convince them it'll turn out okay in the long run."

"Thank you. Anything you can do will help."

Reese decided he liked this agreeable, cooperative side of her. She could be quite accommodating when she put her mind to it. After some small talk they wrapped things up.

"Hold on," Reese said, as Jana was about to hang up. "I'd like to come by on Sunday and pick you up. That way we won't miss each other. We can park someplace close to the starting line."

"Good idea."

"See you on Sunday, then."

"I can't wait."

Chapter 17

"You're the hot urban designer brought in from Baltimore?" the blonde, who was eyeing Reese up and down, gushed. She took a slow sip of champagne and peered coquettishly at him over the top of the flute.

"And you are?"

"Adrienne Butterfield. I'm the architect responsible for designing this place." She waved a hand expansively.

Reese's gaze swept the elegant lobby with its vaulted ceilings and rotunda-like setting.

"Nice work." He meant it. Adrienne had done an interesting job of melding several architectural styles.

After the ribbon-cutting ceremony, guests had been invited into the performance center for cocktails and tours of the facility. Finding the whole event bizarrely fascinating, Reese had tromped in beside Yvonne. He was still getting used to the laid-back manner in which Californians did their thing. The ribbon-cutting ceremony had been billed as a semiformal gathering yet there were few men in suits, he being one of those exceptions.

"So," Adrienne said, her hand on his arm, hanging

on as if he were a buoy, "what I want to know is what you have on Bruce? He passed over local talent, like my ex, to bring you in. Now fess up."

Reese could tell the wine was beginning to talk. Given the number of people around, it seemed strange that Adrienne Butterfield would target him.

"That's a question for Bruce," Reese said diplomatically and chuckled to make it seem as if he was joking. Earlier, he'd spotted the developer in the crowd outside accompanied by his wife, Kitty. Bruce's toady, Seth, had also been with him, of course, accompanied by a woman who might or might not be his wife. It made Reese wonder, and not for the first time, what their relationship actually was.

Yvonne was back from her tour of the facility. She looked none too pleased to see Adrienne attached to his arm and monopolizing his time.

"Hello, Adrienne," she said pleasantly. Apparently they knew each other. "You've outdone yourself. This is quite the feather in your cap."

"Thank you."

Adrienne clinked her wineglass against Yvonne's before draining it dry.

"Where is Tim?" Yvonne asked.

Adrienne hiccupped loudly. "There is no Tim in my life." Reacting to the astonished look on Yvonne's face, she chuckled. "He's here somewhere. We're having one of our usual fights."

She was still holding on to Reese's arm, giggling up at him. "Tim and I have a long history of breaking up and getting back together," Adrienne explained. "I think I mentioned earlier he's a designer just like you. He's done some work for Bruce before, but Bruce passed him over this time around."

In an attempt to move him along, Yvonne linked her arm through Reese's free one. "There's someone I need you to meet, darling. Let's refresh our drinks and find Carlos."

"Carlos, as in Carlos Pinellas, the city manager?" Adrienne asked, wrinkling a nose that reminded Reese of a pug. "Last I knew he was half in the bag. What a waste of time that one is." She relinquished her hold on Reese and sauntered off, twirling her fingers at them.

They found Carlos Pinellas holding court with a group of sycophants. Yvonne quickly made introductions and the usual banalities were exchanged. It soon became obvious that the men without exception had been indulging at the bar.

"Rothschild is over there with his crowd," Carlos brayed, jutting a thumb in the direction of an over-crowded area. "How come you're not with him?"

Reese was not about to be pulled into that type of discussion. "We'll catch up later," he said.

"So how's it going?" one of the men flanking Carlos, who'd been introduced as Dennis Cunningham, asked. "Tell us about these big plans for Lakeview Park."

"I don't know about big plans but there'll be changes," Reese said affably.

"A change has been long overdue," Dennis said. "But try getting that through the people's heads who live in that area. They feel threatened. Just look at the way they're acting, you would think they'd want to get rid of that drug haven."

"I guess there's always some amount of trepidation to be expected." Reese looked around for Yvonne. She was chatting nearby with a woman.

There was a lull in the conversation and Reese took

advantage of it. "I guess Bruce was fortunate to get such a desirable piece of land. I heard it's been leased to the city for years. What made Lakatos decide to sell when the lease came up for renewal is what I'd like to know."

"Could be he needed the money," Cunningham offered, clinking his ice noisily against his glass.

"Nah, Horace has got more money than Donald Trump," another of the drinking buddies offered. "He's just plain weird. All right, Carlos, give us the story. What really happened with Lakatos?"

The city manager took another swig of his drink. "Come on, guys, how can you expect me to remember? I handle so many of these leases every day. Some get renewed. Some don't. That's just the way that it is. I don't recall anything out of the ordinary happening, other than at lease end, Horace Lakatos decided he wanted to sell."

"Did the council get sixty day's notice of intention to not renew the lease?" Yvonne asked, entering in the conversation. "I don't remember, but I know it's customary."

"My dear," Carlos said, placing a hefty arm around Yvonne's shoulders, "you have much too much on your plate. Like me you can't be expected to remember these things. There's Judge Greene, I'm going to go over and hear all about what it's like to be retired."

Taking his buddies with him, Carlos left them.

"Interesting man," Reese said to Yvonne after Carlos was safely out of earshot. "A little overbearing for my taste."

"He's quite popular and he does get the job done."

A hand patted the small of his back causing him to turn. "Reese, is that you?"

A dark-skinned black woman, in an expensively tailored dress and pumps, had come up to him. Her escort was a solidly built white man with a full head of blond hair.

"Mona Davis," she said, sticking her hand out. "Remember me? This is my husband, Gordon."

Jana's mother. Reese smiled, unable to believe his luck. What he liked about Mona was that she didn't seem to care about status. She didn't throw the fact she was a doctor in your face. He'd noticed she hadn't introduced her husband as a doctor either.

In their time together, Jana had barely mentioned that her father was white. And why would she? Not that it mattered to him anyway. He'd just made the assumption that her staunch support of the folks living around the Lakeview area resulted from deep cultural pride. And it might very well have. Except that that pride had been instilled by a black mother and white father.

"I've heard a lot about you," Gordon Davis said, clasping Reese's hand in his and pumping it vigorously. "My wife has been talking about you nonstop since Jana seems to have taken an interest in you."

"I like your daughter very much."

Reese sensed Yvonne, who was now talking to Mona, stiffen.

"Jana is quite the handful, though. Consider yourself warned."

"I'll take that into consideration," Reese said diplomatically.

Yvonne's attempt at conversation stopped. Reese guessed she'd totally tuned in to the conversation. Just as well, maybe now she would realize where his interest lay and that would circumvent any ideas of hitting on him. He'd been planning to tell her he could no longer act as her escort. And he'd not been looking forward to awkward speeches and hurt feelings when they said good night.

Gordon Davis leaned in, confiding, "Mona and I are very happy that our girl seems interested in you. This has been a long time in coming. Our Jana has a history of taking up with the wrong kind of guy: men that are big on causes but don't have much of a portfolio to back their interest up." Gordon touched his arm. "Don't get me wrong, we're not snobs. We just want what's best for Jana. She comes from a good home and we brought her up right. She needs a professional, someone she has something in common with."

"I would imagine every parent wants what's best for their child," Reese said diplomatically.

On the one hand he'd just been complimented, on the other, he'd been put on notice. Gordon was establishing what the expectations were up front and Reese hadn't even taken his daughter out on their second official date.

"I understand perfectly, sir," Reese said, playing the game. "And I couldn't agree with you more." He turned his attention back to Yvonne. Her complexion had visibly reddened though she was still putting up a brave front, smiling politely at Mona.

"Has Gordon been bending your ear?" Mona asked, slipping an arm through her husband's. "My darling does have a tendency to go on when he's on his favorite subject, our daughter. Nice seeing you again, Yvonne," she said, wiggling her fingers at the councilwoman. "Take care, Reese. You're doing the run on Sunday, I hear. We'll be there."

The Davises took off, leaving him with a sober-looking Yvonne.

"What run is this?" she asked after the couple were out of sight.

"It's a charity event to raise money for HIV babies. How's your drink holding up?"

Yvonne held up her glass for Reese's inspection. She'd been sipping on spritzers all evening. Reese had to give her credit for always being professional. These types of outings were business functions to her. Many of the people he'd encountered tonight would have done well to take a leaf out of her book.

"This run," Yvonne said, seemingly fixated on the subject, "sounds interesting and it is for a good cause. I think I'll get my sneakers out and get in on it."

Just what he needed, but what could he say?

"Good idea, Yvonne. As you said it's for a worthwhile cause."

Reese decided to stay as far away from her as possible if she showed up.

Mona considered calling Jana from her cell phone but decided to wait. Jana would resent it if she thought she was sticking her nose in her business. But really, the child should be warned. She needed to know what she was up against.

Since there were no surgeries scheduled for tomorrow and there were only a handful of patients to be seen, Mona considered talking to Gordon about swinging by Jana's place. Her headstrong, independent daughter needed tips on keeping the designer's interest. Maybe she could tactfully suggest a complete makeover.

"Gordon," she said, "how about we pay Jana a surprise visit? It's been a while since we saw her place."

"Another time. I'd really like to get home and relax," Gordon answered, surprising her.

Mona decided to leave it alone. Somehow she would have to convey to Jana that Reese McDonald was a very good catch.

But even long after they'd arrived home, and Gordon was settled with his paper, Mona remained preoccupied.

"You'll wear holes in the tile, darling," Gordon said, eyeing her over the top of the newspaper. "What's got you so unsettled?"

"That Munoz woman, that's what. She's got her eye on Reese. My Jana's a baby next to that barracuda."

"Mind your own business, hon."

"I'm trying."

Mona took a seat on the arm of Gordon's chair. He linked an arm around her stomach and blew a warm breath against her nape. When he started making slow circles with his fingers through the material of her clothes, she slapped his hand away.

"Let me think," Mona said, jumping to her feet again. "Our Jana is so naive she's not going to know how to deal with an experienced shark like Yvonne."

"Shark, barracuda, make up your mind. I wouldn't underestimate Jana if I were you," Gordon said sagely. "I've seen that child in action when she wants something and she's tough as nails."

"Yes, but Yvonne is at least ten years older. She's got clout plus life experience under her belt. That's a formidable combination. Our daughter needs to be put on notice."

"Leave it alone." Gordon's tone brooked no nonsense. "It's time for bed, hon."

"It's only 9:00 PM and you don't have to work tomorrow."

"Exactly."

"I'll be up shortly. I must call Jana."

"Mona!" Gordon warned.

But Mona was already heading for the phone.

Jana had just returned from her pilates class. As usual after each session she felt limber and refreshed. The ringing phone was a shrill reminder that reality was about to return. Winston was still off on a trip somewhere.

After hastily checking the caller ID, Jana picked up the phone.

What was it with her mother these days? Mona's calls were becoming more and more frequent. She seemed to need to make a connection.

"Yes, Mother?" Jana said, patiently.

"How did you know . . .? Ah, yes modern technology. Are you in bed?"

"No, Mother. Was there something you wanted?" Jana asked, getting straight to the point.

"Just calling to fill you in. Let it not be said I'm not looking out for your interest, child."

This was new. It had always been Carmen who'd looked out for her, or so she'd thought.

"I'm becoming concerned about that woman," Mona said in a rush. "You'll need to watch her, she's up to no good."

"What woman?"

"Yvonne Munoz. She was out with Reese tonight."

Silence on the other end before Jana rallied. "Mother," she screamed, "this is really none of your business. Your buying Reese McDonald does not give you license to pry."

Mona, seemingly suitably chastised, responded. "I'm

not trying to pry, sweetheart. I'm just looking out for you."

"And I appreciate that very much but I am twenty-six years old. Old enough to handle my own affairs."

"And young enough to not know what you're dealing with."

"Good night, Mother."

After Mona hung up, Jana reflected on her mother's words. She'd thought Reese was interested in her exclusively and now she was getting a reality check.

Jana had disliked Yvonne the moment she'd laid eyes on her, and that dislike had turned into something else when she'd come sauntering into Judge Greene's retirement party with Reese on her arm.

Now Jana was feeling more annoyed than anything else with herself for being deceived. And she had no right to be. She and Reese had no understanding.

It never occurred to her she might well be jealous.

Chapter 18

Sunday turned out to be a picture-perfect California day: cloudless with little or no humidity in the air. It was the ideal day for the AIDS charity run. Reese normally liked to sleep in on weekends but today he didn't mind rolling out of bed at seven o'clock.

He was exhilarated at the thought of seeing Jana again, and admittedly a little nervous. He was also looking forward to meeting up with her parents again. He found them to be a fascinating couple and it tickled his funny bone that he'd been given their blessing to pursue their daughter.

Reese climbed into Lycra running shorts and a T-shirt before stepping into a tracksuit and Adidas. He grabbed his towel, fanny pack, and water bottle and took off. For a moment he considered warming up by jogging over to Jana's place but quickly reconsidered. He hadn't quite gotten his bearings yet. Who knew how far away from Golden Hill the starting point of the race was? Into the Range Rover he climbed.

In less than five minutes he had a thumb pressed to

Jana's doorbell. She emerged all wide-eyed and scrubbed, her bouncy curls pulled back and secured by a clip. She was wearing a bright red T-shirt with white lettering that said RUN FOR YOUR MONEY and thigh-hugging athletic shorts.

Filling Reese's vision was the picture of the woman whose honey-toned body had lain under him naked, and who'd responded to his touch as if they'd choreographed every move. He could still smell her, hear her, and feel her.

"Morning," she said, handing him a bright yellow T-shirt that matched her own.

"Morning," he answered, feasting his eyes on her.

Back in the Range Rover, Reese shrugged out of the track jacket and yanked off his own shirt, substituting yellow for white.

He thudded an open palm against his forehead. "I should have asked," he said. "There must be some sort of sponsorship associated with this run."

"Yes, but it's all been taken care of. I asked you out so I pay."

"Not where I come from. I was raised to be a gentleman. I pay. Put me down for two hundred bucks."

"But Reese…"

"But Reese nothing. Where's the meeting point anyway?"

Jana told him.

After circling for blocks they were able to find a parking space and followed what seemed like hoards of enthusiastic runners toward the starting line.

It was an interesting assortment of people, ranging in age from young teenagers to seniors in incredible shape. The runners converging were a rainbow of colors reflective of the fact that HIV did not discriminate.

"I thought your parents were supposed to show up," Reese said when they were stretching to warm up.

"They are. But if I know my mother it's doubtful she'll be here at the starting line. She'll join the run at some later point."

Reese didn't know Mona well enough to comment but he was starting to get the picture. There was an underlying animosity between Jana and her mother, something he meant to get to the bottom of. He'd found Jana's mother totally enchanting and admired her guts. A case of the daughter feeling she could not live up to the mother's image, he supposed. Yes, that might produce friction.

Eight o'clock came and went. The runners were getting impatient.

"The sun's really going to be up shortly," one of them complained as he jogged in place.

"Isn't that Yvonne?" Jana asked, elbowing Reese in the ribs. "Does she even run? This is the first time I've seen her at any event that required activity or sweat."

Reese glanced in the direction Jana was looking. Sure enough there was Yvonne in capri pants athletic gear, a sun visor, and sneakers that looked like they'd just come out of the box. Reese thought she looked ridiculous. He hoped that, considering the number of runners, she wouldn't spot him.

Too late, Yvonne was already on her way over.

Jana's intake of breath was audible. Reese placed an arm around her shoulders as she slowly jogged in place. By doing so he hoped to send a very loud and clear message to Yvonne.

Now she was almost on top of them. He felt Jana's shoulders tense up.

"Hi, Reese," Yvonne said, tossing a cursory nod in Jana's direction. "Isn't this a glorious day?"

"The best."

She began running in place and the visor she was wearing began to flop.

"How long is this run?" Yvonne asked Reese, ignoring Jana.

"Ten miles," Jana inserted. "A long way."

Yvonne continued to ignore her. Her full attention was now on Reese.

"That was such fun the other evening," she said. "Usually those things are dreary. I attend so many of those functions, and after a while they all seem the same."

"Yes, it certainly was different." Reese remembered the officials he'd encountered, all of whom seemed to be indulging way too much.

"Carlos Pinellas asked about you." Yvonne's high-pitched laugh rang out. "Actually it was a totally inappropriate question." She chuckled again. "He wanted to know if we were dating."

This time Reese felt Jana flinch. He didn't have to look at her to know her eyes had changed to that dangerous gun-smoke color. His hold around her shoulders tightened. Didn't she know she had nothing to worry about?

"And you said?" he asked.

Yvonne laughed again. A nervous titter. "Of course I told him to mind his business."

"Good for you."

"Reese McDonald. Fancy seeing you here."

The woman's voice came from behind him. Reese released Jana to turn around. His smile brightened as he faced Adrienne Butterfield, accompanied by a lanky man in his forties.

"Hi, Yvonne," Adrienne chirped.

And although she did not look pleased, Yvonne was at least civil.

"Hello, Adrienne, Tim. Glad to see you two together."

"We're never apart for too long. You know that." Tim kissed the top of Adrienne's cap. A blond ponytail streamed from the opening in the back.

"How's it going?" Adrienne said in the direction of Jana although she had yet to be introduced to her.

"Wonderfully well. Look, the run's about to start." Jana pointed in the direction of a man in a bright neon cap at the starting line with a pistol in one hand and a megaphone in the other.

On cue, the man bellowed: "one, two, three, go!" A blank shot exploded in the air and masses of people began running, some banging into each other.

Reese and Jana jockeyed for a comfortable position, almost an impossibility, given the number of runners. Reese hoped he would lose Yvonne but she remained right there next to them. He shot Jana a silent message, one he hoped she'd understand. She raised both eyebrows and picked up the pace. Maybe she'd gotten it.

After a while Yvonne began to slow down. Ten minutes later they'd completely lost her. The sun was high in the sky as the finish line approached. The remaining people, a group that had dwindled drastically, huffed and puffed their way to a victorious finish.

Sweat poured across their faces as Jana and Reese continued jogging to cool down. Someone spritzed them with a water squirter, then handed them towels.

"Great job. Well done," Gordon Davis said from somewhere in their peripheral vision. His T-shirt appeared remarkably dry for a man who was supposed to have been running.

"We can't keep up with you young people," Mona chimed, her practical sunglasses firmly in place. She wore the same T-shirt as her husband did, with the same slogan as Jana and Reese's: RUN FOR YOUR MONEY. It didn't have a wrinkle. "We quit after the first mile."

"You kids need a ride back to your vehicle? You could come to the picnic with us," Gordon suggested.

Jana shot Reese a look but he shook his head.

"Thanks, but we both need showers. How about we catch up with you there?"

"Sounds like a good plan," Gordon said, waving them off.

Gulping air, Jana waved to her parents and circled back the way they had come, Reese at her side.

An hour or so later they were heading to Pacific Beach where the picnic was being held. The laid-back beach town was home to a melting pot of people and the location a perfect one, close to SeaWorld, Old Town, and La Jolla. P.B. was the perfect town to get around on foot or bicycle. But right now traffic was snarled. All vehicles seemed to be heading for the charity picnic.

Finally they found a parking space and began following a crowd toward the Crystal Pier where Jana had told him the bulk of the festivities was to be held. There were plans for kite flying, volleyball, and water sports. There was even a competition to see who could build the best sand castle. There would be something for everyone, with special events for children.

They climbed down steep steps and onto a beach already well populated with people. Colorful umbrellas had been erected as far as the eye could see and children frolicked in the ocean. Off to the side, at the area reserved for barbecuing, a line had already begun to form.

"I suppose we should make an effort to find your parents," Reese suggested. What he really wanted was time alone with Jana. So far they'd not had much time to talk.

"Not right now, maybe later."

He could have kissed her, and in fact wanted to.

"What would you like to do?" he asked.

She gazed at him through her beautiful gray eyes and said, "Take a walk along the beach and get away from all these people."

"Sounds like a capital plan to me."

Reese took her hand and together they walked along the surf and away from the crowd. Finding a spot not frequented by people. Reese finally indulged his fantasy, kissing Jana with a passion that hopefully conveyed how much he'd missed her. He finally released her when he feared things might get out of hand.

Hand in hand they continued to walk. After a while they climbed stairs that led back onto the boardwalk again but at a farther point.

Reese stopped at a kiosk and bought them both bottled water before continuing on.

"What's up with you and Yvonne Munoz?" Jana eventually asked him.

Was she jealous? Reese wasn't certain whether this was a good thing or bad. "Nothing," he answered, leaving it at that.

"You escorted her to Iris Sandifer's party and you were with her at the opening of the performance center. Now she shows up today, alluding that the two of you are dating. Not that it's any of my concern," Jana hastened to add.

"We are not dating." Hopefully that would put an end to any crazy notions.

Jana just stared at him and after a while said, "Then why did Yvonne feel compelled to attend today's run? She's not the type to be seen at these types of events unless there is some publicity to be had. I've never ever seen the woman sweat. Today she was jogging so close to you, your perspiration and hers practically mingled."

"So she has a crush on me, that's hardly my fault. Look, I took Yvonne to the ribbon cutting ceremony of the performance art center because I wanted to meet Carlos Pinellas, that's all."

"Who's that?"

"Carlos is the city manager and the person responsible for making sure the council is aware of leases that should be renewed."

"And Carlos had to know that the Lakeview Park lease was in danger of expiring."

"Exactly. It doesn't sound right to me that the city would walk away from a lease that they'd been renewing since the fifties. Bruce scooped up that property because he got wind of the situation early."

Jana scrunched up her nose, clearly thinking. "Sounds like an inside leak to me. Someone on the city council must have tipped him off."

"That's what I've been thinking. But I'd be curious to find out why they decided not to renew the lease. There had to be some reason . . . Let's head back."

"What does Yvonne have to say?" Jana asked, taking Reese's hand as they began walking back along the boardwalk.

"She doesn't remember the issue coming up."

"How could that be?"

Reese shrugged. "I don't know but I sure mean to find out. I'm thinking there might be some way to get the property owner, Horace Lakatos to talk to me."

"I know how you can," Jana said excitedly. She was practically bubbling over with glee. "Carmen's sister is his housekeeper. She can ask him if he would at least agree to call."

"Who's Carmen?"

"My parents' housekeeper. She used to be my nanny way back when."

"And she wouldn't mind asking her sister to inquire whether Horace would speak to me?"

"Carmen will pretty much do anything for me."

"And so will I."

This time Reese kissed her in front of what had to be hundreds of weekenders on the crowded board-walk.

His admission had stunned him. He'd never fully experienced what it was like to be emotionally intimate with a woman before, but he was sure this came damn close to being it.

"I say we go get some good Latino home cooking," Jana suggested when she came up for air. "And I know just the place. We'll go to my parents' home and you can meet Carmen."

Chapter 19

"A Ken Gibson's on the phone for you," the receptionist at Planned Parenthood said when Jana picked up the intercom.

"Put him through."

For Ken to call her at her office meant something was up.

"What's happening?" Jana asked the moment he greeted her.

"I need you," he said. "Can you come by today?"

"Why?"

"The natives are getting restless. I'm hearing rumors of a sit-in in front of the center."

"What's got the group riled up now?" Jana asked.

Ken groaned. "Someone spotted a couple of contractors on the premises and began asking questions. Now of course the rumors are spreading and the community is presuming it's only a matter of time before construction begins."

"Are the rumors true?"

"Who knows?" Ken answered, sounding totally aggravated. "What I do know is that these folks are out of control and there's no reasoning with them. That's why I need your help."

Jana eyed the clock on her office wall. She had a full day ahead and it would be at least another couple of hours before she could break free. It was not normally one of the days that she would go to the center and in fact she'd made dinner plans with Winston, whom she hadn't seen in days. Lately they'd been like ships passing in the night.

"I'll get there as soon as I can," Jana promised, "and see what I can do about quieting them down."

She hung up the phone, got out her cell, and punched in Reese's programmed number.

After several rings he picked up.

"Hey, babe."

Jana's eyebrows shot sky-high. My, he'd gotten comfortable. "I meant to call and thank you for lunch," he said easily, "but you beat me to it. That's quite the house your parents have and Carmen was delightful. Any word from her sister?"

"Not yet. What's going on with the Lakeview property?"

"What do you mean 'What's going on'?"

"Ken tells me there's been contractors walking the property."

"They're allowed," Reese said.

It was not what Jana wanted to hear. "So you knew about this?"

"Not specifically but it's fairly standard."

"What you're saying is there's been a date set for groundbreaking and work is moving ahead."

"I'm not saying that at all," Reese said warily. "You're in a very argumentative mood this afternoon, darling, and here I was about to invite you to dinner at my place."

That stopped her. Winston wouldn't die if she canceled, especially if she told him she'd gotten a better offer from Reese. But given her promise to Ken she wasn't sure how late she would be.

"It'll have to be after I get done at the center. I've just been summoned by Ken, which means there's trouble afoot."

Reese groaned. "Please, the community needs to ease up. You'll definitely need a drink and something to fortify you when you're done. I'm not going to be done with work until after seven anyway, so how about you drive over to my place at eight thirty and we'll have a bite together. Maybe I'll even cook."

"Great. I'll call Carmen and see if she's talked to her sister about you contacting Horace."

Feeling happier than she'd been before picking up the phone, Jana disconnected.

Afterward she saw a succession of people. Thankfully her last appointment of the day was a no-show and she was able to make it over to Lakeview Park earlier than she'd thought, beating rush-hour traffic.

As she dashed across the parking lot and toward the community center, Jana noticed the people seated outside. Some held signs that voiced their feelings about the development group.

Parked at the curb was a television van with a crew already in motion.

"What's going on?" Jana asked a couple of the boxers.

"We're not moving until someone tells us something."

"Hasn't Ken spoken to you?" Jana asked the crowd in general.

"No, he has not," Hugh Pilgrim, the old man who'd been arrested, said in a wobbly voice.

"That man is useless," someone else shouted.

And although Jana agreed she held her tongue. She fought her way inside the building and stormed into Ken's office. He was on the phone.

Jana tapped four fingers against her open palm, giving him the sign for time out.

Ken was saying something about security needing to be sent for before he hung up.

"Why do you need security?" Jana demanded.

"You saw for yourself. They're wild and out of control."

"Hardly. What these concerned citizens need is to be treated like people. You're, the executive director, you should be giving them updates. What have they been told?"

"I know about as much as they do: nada," Ken said sheepishly.

"Not good enough. Have you called Bruce Rothschild directly? What about putting in an appearance so they don't feel abandoned or thrown to the wolves?"

Ken stood. "And have them jump all over me? This is a mean group, look how they goaded Rothschild into losing it. I don't want my face smeared all over the evening news."

"Well you've got to do something," Jana said, taking Ken by the arm. "I spoke to Reese McDonald before I came over. He doesn't know a thing about a groundbreaking either and if anyone should know, he would."

"Well that's a relief." Ken sighed loudly. "Maybe if I told them that, it would settle them down and I could go home."

"You might try it. And by the way, don't even think

of heading home and leaving me alone. I'm a volunteer," Jana reminded Ken, "and even though I'm terribly concerned, this situation is really not my responsibility."

"I know that."

"The crowd's waiting to hear something," Jana reminded Ken.

"Oh, okay, all right, but you will come with me."

"I suppose."

Jana couldn't believe what a wuss Ken Gibson was.

Eight thirty had come and gone and there was still no sign of Jana. Reese had hoped she would have gotten to his home when it was still light enough to appreciate what he'd done with the garden.

Luckily, at the last minute and largely because he had no idea what time he'd get home, he'd decided to order in rather than cooking. Now even the Indian food, still secured in its quart-size containers, was getting cold. Reese set the table using freshly rinsed plates taken from a box he'd just unpacked.

Using the last of the rapidly dimming light to his advantage, he snipped a couple of roses in full bloom and added trailing ferns to the posy, returning to set it down in the middle of the dining room table before going into the kitchen.

To pass the time he turned on the television set and began surfing channels. Remote in hand, he paused as the name Lakeview Park popped up in the corner of the screen for those who were hearing-impaired. Reese adjusted the volume.

Seated on the curb and sidewalk in front of the center were several faces he recognized. There were signs with derogatory sayings, directed for the most part at the Rothschild organization, although a few seemed to be aimed specifically at him. "The Tom" that the signs referred to didn't need much interpretation.

Ken Gibson paced back and forth, looking totally bewildered and at times lost. The camera panned in on him, replaying a stilted speech he had given, which only seemed to make things worse. There was a close-up of the park's security force, if that's what you could call them, standing by. People screamed profanities and the elderly waved their fists. There was also a fleeting shot of Jana bending over to give one or another of the dissidents a hug.

No wonder she was late. Lakeview Park was taking precedence again.

Reese drummed the tips of his fingers against the tile counters. Things had gotten way out of hand. The public's sympathy must already be with these poor people and Bruce was doing nothing so far to calm down the situation.

Reese's cell phone jingled. Must be Jana telling him she was running late or maybe canceling. But when he glanced at the caller ID he did not recognize the incoming number.

"This is Reese."

"Am I catching you at a bad time?" a high-pitched voice, sounding slightly giddy, asked.

"No, but I'm about to have dinner soon." The last was said in the event he needed an out.

Laughter peeled through the earpiece. "You don't have any idea who you're talking to do you? It's Yvonne."

The woman never gave up. Reese waited for her to continue.

"I've got good news, in fact the best. All of your permits got approved. I pulled some strings."

Reese closed his eyes. His fingers pinched his nose bridge. Was he supposed to say "thank you"? Yvonne was the last person he wanted to be beholden to.

"What exactly did you do?" he asked, keeping his voice even.

"Used my contacts."

The doorbell rang. Ironic. He was literally being saved by the bell.

"I'm sorry, Yvonne, I have to go. My company's here," Reese said, disconnecting before she could get another word out.

He went to the door and pressed an eye to the peephole just to be sure. It was hard to miss those blond-tipped curls. Yanking the door open he embraced Jana.

"Long day, huh?"

"Yes, very long." She rested her head on his chest for a brief moment.

"I saw some of it on television," Reese said, leading her into the kitchen. "It didn't look good."

"It wasn't. Ken made a real mess of things."

He waited until she was seated and without asking poured her a glass of red wine.

"What did Ken say or not say?"

Somehow it didn't come as a surprise that Ken would have bungled things. The man had zero people skills.

"He made the situation worse, got everyone all riled up. I think he got nervous when people started hurling questions at him. As you know that group is easily ignited and they started throwing things. Security was called. It took all I had to get things settled down."

"So how did you leave it?"

Jana sighed. "I'm not sure. I stayed as long as I

could. A few diehards were insistent they would camp out in front of the center all night until they got answers."

Reese shook his head before speaking out loud. "That's not good. It's bound to tick Bruce off. He's going to hate all the adverse publicity. My guess is that things will move quickly now that all the permits have come through."

Jana regarded him through worried gray eyes. "When did this happen?"

"I just found out. Yvonne Munoz called just minutes before you arrived. I'll make a point of talking to Bruce tomorrow."

Reese began dishing out food.

"I hope you like Indian," he said. "I didn't think to ask."

"Love it. What is that—lamb Vindaloo and dahl? Didn't you say you were going to cook?"

"I decided to save my gourmet efforts for another day when I get home at a reasonable time."

Reese poured more wine into both of their glasses. He was pleased when Jana finished every last bite. She shared the same love of Indian cuisine as he did.

After dinner, they sat outdoors on the patio having tea. After a while, when they'd run out of small talk, he sensed Jana was getting restless and probably wanted to go home.

"Why don't you stay with me tonight?" he asked impulsively.

"I have no clothes."

"You practically live around the corner," he reminded her.

"I have a roommate," she countered.

Reese laughed. "You've got to be kidding. I've met Winston. He would probably applaud your decision."

He was at her side, fingers looped around her wrists, gently easing her out of the seat. "Let's take a stroll around the gardens before we call it a night. The gardenias smell wonderful this time of year."

And although she had not agreed to spend the night with him, she walked with him down the steps and onto the sloping back lawn. Reese had had lighting strategically positioned under some trees. He planned to do a lot more landscape architecture when he had the time. Manual labor relaxed him.

He placed an arm loosely around Jana's shoulders as he squired her about. "So what do you think?"

"I think you did a lot of work."

"Glad you noticed."

He stopped in front of some rose bushes that he'd just begun to prune and ran a finger along her jaw. "Have I told you how much you fascinate me?" he asked.

"I bet that's what you say to all the women," she flirted back.

"There haven't been that many," Reese admitted.

"Oh, come now. Men like you aren't that easy to find or at least that's what my mother keeps reminding me."

"What's with you and your mother anyway?"

"I love my mother," Jana said softly, "even though she's self-centered."

"How self-centered? She seems very devoted to you. So, as a matter of fact, does your father."

"My mother seems devoted because she'd like to clone me into her image."

"So that's the problem," Reese said, squeezing her

hand. "You don't think you could live up to her expectations. Hence the avant-garde clothes and the free-spirit image."

"I don't want to live up to anyone's expectations. I can barely live up to mine."

Reese realized he'd struck a nerve. Jana at times came across as a tough cookie but deep down she was as vulnerable as the next person. Clearly, there were some serious issues between her and her mother that she needed to work through.

He would do anything to take away that hurt. He'd been there, except his issues had been different. What he wouldn't have done to have a mother— good, bad, or indifferent. The feelings of abandonment still lingered, the fear of becoming too attached. And he was beginning to become too attached to Jana Davis. That could only lead to hurt.

Still, he couldn't help reaching over and cupping her chin and tilting it upward. He couldn't help covering her lips and drinking deeply of her sweetness, and he couldn't help filling her mouth with his tongue or exploring the grooves and recesses of a mouth that excited him. Just the feel of Jana made him want to make love to her right there.

She kissed him back with wild abandon. Her arms slipped around his waist as they took turns feasting from each other. Reese inhaled Jana's perfumed hair. The sweet fragrance mingled with that of gardenia.

Jana began playing with the buttons on his shirt, unbuttoning them. She slid a hand through his chest hairs and splayed her fingers across his chest. He covered her hand with his, enjoying the warmth of her palm against his skin.

A spasm of desire spiraled through him as she slid

her hand lower to cover his stomach, then inched her way beneath his waistband. Swathes of material from the skirt she wore found their way into his hands as he tugged up the skirt and placed both palms against her bottom, pressing her into him.

When they both swayed, and were in danger of falling, Reese brought her with him to lean against the trunk of a nearby palm tree. He ground his erection into her and Jana wound her arms around his neck. Their breathing, although erratic, eventually synchronized.

Reese could feel Jana's nipples through the thin fabric of the cotton shirt she'd knotted at her waist. His hand dipped into the gap that had been left by the two little buttons that had popped open exposing her ample cleavage. His lips trailed a moist path down her neck and settled in the hollow above her clavicle.

Jana had one arm around his waist and the other inside his pants where she stroked a blooming erection. Reese's hand dipped inside the thong panties she wore and found her throbbing center.

She put space between them to remove her panties and kick them out of her way. Reese got to his knees worshiping her, laving her. After a while Jana shuddered and her sweet juices flowed into his mouth. He freed himself, got to his feet, put on a condom, and entered her. The palm tree trunk provided them support as he entered and exited, dipped, circled, and brought gasps of pleasure to her lips. Then he picked her up and, still impaled, Jana wrapped her thighs around his waist and squeezed.

Reese inhaled, a loud, agonizing breath that represented both pleasure and agony. Relief was only a short while away, he knew. He continued to pump. In and out and in again.

Jana's breath came in short, little bursts. Her fists pummeled his back as she rode him fiercely. She was crying out, urging him on.

"Come with me," she called in a breathy voice.

And he was coming with her, matching her spurt for spurt and gasp for gasp. Together, their bodies spiraled out of control.

Chapter 20

"What do you mean you've padlocked the doors to the community center?" Reese asked. It took every bit of restraint he had to remain on his side of Bruce's desk.

"Why not? I own the property. The permits are approved and these people have proven to be nothing but nuisances."

"Do you realize the kind of turmoil you'll cause? The reporters will have a field day."

"They've already had their field day," Bruce said, looking as if Reese had already taken up too much of his time. "I don't think there's anything left to say about me or my ethics that hasn't been said."

True, but this was not the way to win public sympathy. Reese had tried diplomatically to tell Bruce that. So far he was getting nowhere.

"Have you had time to look at the revised designs?" Reese asked, shifting the conversation.

"I did."

"And what do you think?"

"I'll okay the green, and a few biking paths, even the botanical gardens. There's money to be made if we charge an entry fee. Forget the fishing piers, that's using up good dock space. I don't want that kind of element around when people go to use their boats."

"That's a compromise of sorts," Reese said carefully. "I'm not sure how well it will go over, but at least it's something."

Bruce had already picked up a pen and was now sifting through some papers. "By the way," he said, deigning to raise his head, "as soon as construction begins we're leveling the community center."

"Why?"

"Because that will take care of the whining. Let them find some other place to go. I don't need anyone around obstructing the developmental process."

"I think you're making a huge mistake," Reese answered. "At least give the folks some notice. Give them three months so that they can find another center nearby. Don't just go in and demolish a building that means so much to them."

"The decision's already made," Bruce snapped, his tone brooking no nonsense. "I'm breaking ground in two weeks and that's that."

"Okay, I'm sure you know best."

But Reese wasn't so sure the developer did know best. In fact he would bet Bruce had no idea the events he'd just set in motion.

"That nanny of yours called," Winston said as Jana came through the front door. "She wants you to call her back. She says you have her number."

"Carmen's looking for me?"

"That would be the only nanny I know."

Jana set down her files on the coffee table and headed for the phone.

"Are you all right?" she asked the minute her parents' housekeeper picked up.

"Not to worry, *chica.* I am fine. Maria got back to me. She says to let your *amor* know Mr. Lakatos is expecting his call. Let me give you the number."

Carmen rattled off a phone number, which Jana quickly recorded.

Jana's next move was to call Reese. She was conscious of Winston openly listening and felt relief when Reese's voice mail kicked in. She quickly left a message including Horace's number.

"Jana! Jana!" Winston said behind her. "Looks like there's trouble brewing big-time."

She spun around facing the television set that Winston was crouched down next to. He was turning the volume up. The same reporter who'd commented during the sit-in was now babbling excitedly.

" . . .And the developer, Bruce Rothschild, having had enough, has padlocked the doors of the community center." The camera panned to another scene, showing groups of people mobbing the building, some angrily trying to break the locks.

The microphone was then thrust into the faces of those most vocal. A series of beeps indicated when profanity was being censored. A lot of anger and bitterness came spewing forth. The community took this as a personal affront.

Jana stood there, arms supporting a stomach that hurt. Reese had to have known something about this. He had to know what Bruce was planning to do; yet he'd never said one word. Jana felt used, angry, and betrayed.

This latest development made her wonder if his interest in her was real. Maybe she'd been the means by which he'd gotten information to report back to Bruce. Perhaps he'd wanted insight into the psyche of the Lakeview community people she'd helped.

The scene on-screen was an outrage. The police had once again been called in and people were being carted off by the carload. Jana saw a dark-haired teenager being shoved into the back of a cop car. The girl looked a lot like Lucy Santana.

"Is that a live shot?" Jana asked Winston.

"Yes, baby girl, as live as it gets."

Jana picked up her purse. "I'll need to get down to the center and find out what's going on."

"Be careful," Winston shouted after her, right before she slammed the front door.

Reese turned on his cell phone to discover he had messages. He'd been in conference with Bruce and Seth earlier and a ringing or vibrating phone would have been an unwelcome distraction.

In front of the building, he punched in the programmed numbers for voice mail and listened to a succession of messages, many of which did not require an immediate return call. Then Jana's voice resonated in his ear and he smiled to himself.

It felt good knowing she'd called him. It felt even better being on the verge of a relationship with a woman who excited him on every level. Jana was his intellectual equal, and a woman courageous enough to maintain her individuality. Reese knew he would never be bored. Jana was everything he'd hoped for and more.

And she'd come through for him, getting him Horace Lakatos's telephone number, which he quickly programmed into his cell, and then called.

In seconds, a wobbly male voice came on the line. The person on the other end sounded ancient.

"Lakatos," he greeted. "Who is this?"

"Reese McDonald. Maria, your housekeeper, said you'd be expecting my call."

"Yes, she mentioned you would call. What is it you want?"

The old man was direct and to the point. What did he want? Answers perhaps.

Reese explained his role in designing the park. He explained to Horace that he often contacted the original property owner to discuss what he envisioned doing with the land.

That seemed to please the old man to be included.

"I'm a naturalist," he said. "That park's been in my family for years. It was originally a wildlife preserve. I spent hours as a teenager exploring the grounds and hiding out from my parents when it came time for another stiff sit-down dinner."

"It sounds to me like there are some very fond memories associated with that land," Reese said.

"Yes, there are. But it seemed so selfish after my parents died, keeping all that acreage for myself when there were people who would benefit from spending time outdoors."

"So you leased it to the city?"

"I did."

"And for some reason, which no one seems to know, you decided not to renew your lease this year."

"What are you talking about?"

Bingo!

"I'm talking about the fact that rather than renew the lease you chose to sell to a developer."

"Whoa. Wait a minute. I didn't want to sell," Horace

said, sounding baffled. "It was the city that chose not to renew the lease. They never even had the courtesy of giving me an explanation. I called numerous times but no one would speak to me."

"And you sold to Bruce Rothschild because?"

"Because he contacted me. He said he'd always been interested in the property and that he would find usage for the space that would be beneficial to those less fortunate. I wasn't looking to make a killing. Frankly, I don't need the money. I sold Rothschild that land cheap."

"Thank you for letting me know that," Reese said. "If I were you, I'd dig a little and see why the Lakeview lease wasn't renewed. It might all have been a misunderstanding."

"Too late now," Horace said sagely. "But I'd be interested in your plans for the acreage. There's been so much controversy in the news, I'm almost sorry I sold the property to begin with."

Reese thanked the old man again and disconnected the call. He took his time walking to the parking lot. He'd smelled a rat from the very beginning and he had the feeling the rat's last name began with a *P*. Reese had had dealings with City Hall frequently but most of the people he interacted with were in an administrative capacity. He needed someone with real clout to look into what might be an oversight. But Reese had the sneaking suspicion this wasn't the case.

His only good contact at the city was Yvonne Munoz and even though that meant calling her again, he had no choice. The situation required some delicacy, and he might even have to eat crow. He decided to put off making that phone call until tomorrow.

Reese climbed into the Range Rover and took off.

His thoughts vacillated between this new development and what to do about Jana. He'd realized after their last lovemaking session that she'd really gotten under his skin and he was dangerously close to falling in love with her. It was a scary reality for a man who'd vowed to never get too attached.

And although he'd promised himself to wait a day or two before calling Jana, he found his fingers punching in her programmed number. His excitement heightened in anticipation of hearing her voice and quickly dissipated when voice mail kicked in.

Reese hurriedly left a message, hoping that he came over as caring and interested in hearing from her. This uncertainty, this lack of confidence, was an entirely new feeling. It mattered very much to him what Jana now thought.

On the drive home he mulled over his earlier conversation with Bruce. The developer was taking this situation with the Lakeview Park community much too personally. His decision to lock out the people seemed way over the top. As much as it was quite the coup to be the designer on a project of this magnitude, Reese was tempted to chuck it in. There were other projects out there for a designer with a reputation like his.

Sure Bruce had offered a compromise of sorts, but it didn't amount to much. A green, a handful of bicycle paths, and a garden the community would have to pay an entrance fee to would be viewed as an insult. It would be like putting a Band-Aid on an already festering wound.

What he needed to do was find out why the city had chosen not to renew the lease on a park they'd had access to for sixty-odd years. Reese might then have something to hold over Bruce's head that would force him to come around to his own way of thinking.

Reese glanced at the digital clock on his vehicle's dashboard. He might still be able to catch Yvonne in her office. Attorneys kept long hours. If she didn't answer he'd try her cell phone.

He actually felt a pang of guilt that he might shamelessly be using the woman but quickly got over it. He hadn't misled Yvonne. If she wanted to put a spin on his initiating this call, then so be it. With one hand, he rifled through the wallet that he'd tucked into the cup holder, and removed a stack of business cards. Taking his eyes off the road momentarily, he plucked one from the pile that he thought might be the councilwoman's.

Yup, he'd gotten lucky. Digit by digit he plunked in the numbers. The phone rang and then an automated voice requested he leave a message. Was everyone on voice mail today?

Reese had no choice but to try Yvonne's cell phone number. She picked up on the third ring.

"Hello there," she said, chirpy as ever.

Caller ID again. He was busted

Reese politely inquired as to Yvonne's well-being. After exchanging banalities, he opted for the direct approach.

"I had an interesting conversation with Horace Lakatos," he began.

"Lakatos, as in the railroad heir? The man who sold the Lakeview property to Bruce?" Yvonne sounded puzzled.

"Yes, that would be him."

"Is there some problem?"

He had to give Yvonne credit; if nothing else, she was astute.

"Well, it seems Horace tells a very different story from the one you and I understood. According to the old man, the city chose not to renew the lease on the Lakeview property. Horace says he sold the acreage because he had no use for it. Bruce apparently told him the land would be utilized for the benefit of the people."

"I don't remember any discussion of that lease coming up for renewal," Yvonne muttered more to herself than to him. "All I remember hearing is that the owner was going to sell to a private party. I'll give Iris Sandifer a call and see what she knows. She's the city attorney, the woman who threw the party for her boyfriend, Judge Greene. And I'll talk to Carlos Pinellas. It's his job to make sure all leases up for renewal are brought to the attention of the council."

It came back to Carlos again.

"Has it happened before where a lease slipped through the cracks?" Reese asked.

There was a very long pause on the other end before Yvonne said, "Sure, situations do happen. This would be huge, though. We're talking a park here and an entire community has been affected. What are you doing later this evening by the way?"

Not again. He needed to think quickly.

"Heading for an appointment." Not true but not exactly a lie either.

"That's disappointing. I was hoping we could get together."

Maybe it was time to deal with the issue.

"Yvonne," Reese said, "things are getting pretty serious between me and Jana Davis."

"That little girl, the caterer?"

Yvonne's words dripped of disdain. She made it

sound as if Jana was beneath her and him and she was by far superior.

"That little girl is twenty-six years old and happens to have a master's degree in social work. She also has a business of her own. And I like her very much."

Yvonne sniffed. "So is this an exclusive arrangement?"

"Left to me, it will be."

He felt so much better for saying that.

"I see," Yvonne grunted, clearly put out.

Mumbling something about having to go, she quickly disconnected the call.

Chapter 21

Jana arrived to find the grounds in front of the community center swarming with reporters, cops, and onlookers. Police cars and armed cops blocked access to the building itself. She watched helplessly as several people were led away.

A well-known black activist was spouting rhetoric at several television cameras. Where in the world was Ken? He'd asked her to be here and he was nowhere in sight.

Jana approached a police officer and handed him her business card and photo-ID badge, identifying her as a social worker.

"I need to get into the community center," she said, asserting herself.

The cop gave a cursory look at her card and badge and handed it back to her. "Sorry, no one's allowed inside the building."

"But I was asked by Ken Gibson, the center's executive director, to come down here. He said I was needed to help."

"Hey, Prince," the officer shouted at another cop. "You know someone called Ken Gibson?"

Prince shaded his eyes and looked at Jana. "Can't say that I do. Wait a second. I wonder if that's the guy Constantino hauled down to the station and booked."

Not Ken. He had to be mistaken. Ken, the wimp, would never have been in the middle of the action. He would have been hiding out in that office of his.

Jana saw a couple of people she recognized standing off to the side. One of them was Drew, who'd gotten out on bail with the rest of the crowd.

Jana walked over and tugged on the sleeve of his T-shirt. His face registered surprise when he saw her.

"Are you here because of Lucy?" he asked.

"What about Lucy?"

"Don't you know? She mouthed off to one of the cops and they carted her off hours ago."

Jana simultaneously sighed and rolled her eyes. So the dark-haired girl Jana had seen on TV being led off by the cops really *was* Lucy. The teenager just didn't seem able to stay out of trouble.

"Have you seen Ken?" she asked.

"He got hauled off in the back of a police car too," Drew said, this time looking slightly amused. "My boys and I thought it was funny."

"What did Ken do?"

"Nothing. Bad timing. He came out when people started getting destructive. They were throwing rocks and breaking windows. He tried to stop them. One thing led to another. You know how that goes. More stuff's liable to go down when it gets dark."

Jana thanked him and turned away. Something clearly needed to be done. What? Over her dead body would she call Reese . . . not that he could do anything anyway.

Padlocking the community center had been a huge mistake. What it had done was set into action a chain of events, none necessarily good. She was angry that she'd allowed herself to be taken in and manipulated. Now what she needed to do was to figure out how she could get Lucy Santana out of jail. Ken had the means to bail himself out. Lucy had nothing and no one.

While she hated to have to do it, she'd need to seek the advice of her father once again, and she might even have to depend again on his largesse.

Jana fished out her cell phone and noticed the message symbol. Either the phone had not rung or the noise surrounding her had made it virtually impossible to hear the ring. The message might be important. It could very well be Lucy making that one phone call she was allowed.

Jana accessed voice mail, punched in her password, and waited. The first message was from Reese and although her insides wobbled like Jell-O she willed herself to be still. Reese sounded so normal and so sincere, no wonder she'd been taken in by him. Who would have thought this man she'd begun to have feelings for would betray her trust?

Like hell she would call him back. She wanted nothing to do with him. He had balls. She moved on to the next message from her boss at Planned Parenthood. This one was succinct yet urgent. Darlene Harding wanted to see her first thing tomorrow. That meant only one thing: she was in trouble. Could the day get any worse? Jana snapped the flip phone shut and shoved it back into her purse.

For the first time in a long time she felt the over-whelming need to go back to the home she grew up in, take two aspirins, and curl up in bed. It was times like now she needed Carmen.

With the police in charge, there was nothing further to be accomplished at the park. Jana headed for her car and decided that rather than trying to reach her father, who might or might not be at the hospital, she would take that ride to La Jolla.

The entire trip went by in a blur. Each time she felt herself tear up, Jana put it down to a stress-filled day that had left her on edge. She refused to entertain the idea that the sharp stabs of pain jabbing at her gut had anything to do with Reese, or her feelings of betrayal. Jana refused to acknowledge that she actually had feelings for the man. Deep feelings.

She'd driven by rote and was already at her parents' home. She still had her key on the key ring. Jana let herself in and tentatively called, "Anyone home?"

Bourbon, who'd picked up her scent, whined from his igloo in the backyard before beginning an excited series of yaps.

Thinking no one was home, Jana headed for the staircase and her bedroom on the second floor. She was too exhausted to even think about eating. And there was still the matter of Lucy. It was doubtful that her aunt Teresa was in any position to bail her out.

"Jana," Mona called from the landing above. "What a nice surprise. We weren't expecting you."

"Hello, Mother. Is Dad home as well?"

She needed to get to that bedroom and lie down and think. A little solitude would help her sort out the jumbled thoughts converging in her head.

"No, he's still working, I'm afraid," Mona answered. I've been watching the television coverage about Lakeview. What a mess. Bruce Rothschild's actions seem so harsh. All he's succeeded in doing is garnering more sympathy for the community group's cause."

"Yes, I know. I've been in the thick of it for most of the evening."

"No wonder you look exhausted. The last I saw on television some of the more prominent lawyers banded together and volunteered their services. Pretty much everyone who's been arrested has already been released."

That at least was good news. Jana hoped that Lucy was amongst that group.

"Have you had dinner?" Mona asked, meeting Jana halfway on the staircase.

"No, I haven't had time."

"Honey, Carmen made rice, beans, and plantains. I know chicken's out of the question. There's leftovers in the refrigerator. Since I'm off duty for the next two days we can share a glass of wine and catch up."

Mona was reaching out more and more lately. What was this sudden need for a connection? It hadn't seemed all that important when Jana was growing up.

"Yes, I suppose I should eat something," Jana said, retracing her steps. "Give me a second. I need to make a quick phone call."

With some assistance from the operator, and a lot of going back and forth, Jana was finally able to connect with Lucy's aunt Teresa.

"*Sí, sí.* Lucy was not kept in jail. The *abogado*—in English how you say it? Yes, the lawyer—got Lucy out. I went and got her, me and that new boyfriend, and his mama. She is spending the night at the mother's home."

Carmen again to the rescue, like the woman didn't have problems of her own. Another quick call assured Jana that Lucy was indeed with Carmen and her brood.

Jana returned to the kitchen to find Mona had set a

place at the island counter and had already poured wine. She removed a plate from the microwave and set it down on the mat. The aroma wafting over made Jana's stomach growl. Mona joined her on the opposite stool.

Jana's cell phone rang before she could take the first bite. She should have shut it off. She glanced at the dial, recognized Reese's number, and hit a button, popping the call into voice mail. Right now she was too disgusted to deal with him.

"Problem?" Mona asked, surprisingly perceptive.

"Nothing I can't handle."

"How are things coming along with that nice young man?"

Mona either had ESP or Jana's expression had been very revealing.

"They're not coming along right now. I'm very angry."

Mona sipped her wine and waited. Jana managed to shovel down several more forkfuls of Carmen's delicious food.

"Relationships are complicated," Mona said wisely. "At the beginning things didn't go that smoothly between Gordon and me."

That was a surprising admission. Jana had always thought, with the exception of the color issue, things had gone along smoothly, with an adoring Gordon kissing the ground Mona walked on.

"How so?" she asked.

"Well for one, as you know, we were both medical students, busy with studies. I had a job as well, which I needed to help pay tuition. But Gordon seemed to think his time was more important than mine. So we fought."

"How did it get resolved?"

"I kept begging, pleading for us to spend more time together. Then I stopped."

Jana was totally fascinated. She continued to eat, waiting. "And . . ." she said, when Mona showed no signs of continuing.

"Well, when Gordon thought my interest was waning, he began turning up the heat. The bouquets of flowers started arriving, the phone calls increased. And when he found out that I had a study partner, male of course, he was beside himself. Amazingly he found time to fit me in."

"But isn't that game-playing, Mother?"

Mona looked at her wide-eyed. Her voice was smooth as silk when she continued. "No, it's called self-preservation, strategizing, and maintaining your self-esteem. In matters of the heart, no one should be more important than you are. When you feel someone is treating you with less respect than you deserve, then it's time to put your foot down."

"This isn't about a lack of respect. This is about feeling deceived," Jana admitted. "This is about me feeling used."

"Ah. Now that's serious. Would Yvonne Munoz be playing a role in these feelings?"

"Not really."

Jana went on to tell her mother she suspected Reese knew about the lockout yet he'd never said a word.

"He may not have," Mona said sagely. "And the only way you'll know is to ask him directly in person, and watch his reaction. You're a social worker, you're good at reading people."

Mona surprised her by climbing off the stool and giving her a hug.

"I'm in your corner, baby. I've always been in your

corner. And yes, I know there have been times I've allowed work to get in the way. But be assured that your father and I love you very much."

It was a huge admission and long overdue in coming. It made Jana tear up. Maybe Mona wasn't as cold and remote as she'd thought her to be while she was growing up. And maybe the distance she'd put between herself and her mother had all been more or less her doing.

When it had come down to it, both parents had always been there for her.

"Jana, I'm not sure if your cell phone is working. I've left you a number of messages. Please call me if you get this message."

Perplexed, Reese disconnected the call. He wasn't sure what was going on. It had been several days now since he'd had any contact with Jana. In that time he must have left at least eight messages, none of which had been returned. His next and final attempt would be to try reaching her on her home phone.

Reese paced the length of the conference room where he'd established an office. More often than not he was getting into small disagreements with Bruce. The developer would no longer entertain the thought of affordable housing. Even medium-priced housing was out of the question now. Bruce had taken the comments and threats made by the Lakeview community personally. He was unwilling to pacify the group beyond giving them the token biking paths and green.

As a result, Reese was not getting the usual pleasure out of putting the finishing touches on his designs. He'd had such hope and such vision for Lakeview Park. Now all his plans were predicated on the developer's need to send a loud and very clear message to the folks who'd stood up to him.

Reese had discretely started looking around for other opportunities in the San Diego vicinity. He liked the area and especially the climate and the laid-back California lifestyle. He'd made up his mind, lucrative or not, this was the last project he'd work on for Bruce Rothschild. The man's ethics were far different from his.

"Reese?"

The female voice startled him. Yvonne was the last person he'd expected to see here. As usual the helmet-like hair created a halo effect. She strode across the conference room in sensible black pumps.

"Good afternoon, Yvonne."

She took his arm. "Is there someplace we could go to talk? Preferably not in the building."

Her tone sounded serious. Reese sensed whatever she had to discuss was not necessarily some trumped-up ploy to get him off in a secluded corner.

"There's a Starbucks across the street," he offered.

"That'll do."

Reese accompanied her out of the building.

When they were seated across from each other with cups of coffee in hand Yvonne quietly said, "You were right about the Lakeview Park lease, Reese."

Her announcement got his full attention. "What did you find out?"

"According to Carlos, when confronted, it was an oversight. He misread the lease date."

Reese hiked an eyebrow. "The council believes him?"

Yvonne looked like she'd digested something sour. "After the situation was discovered, a decision was made to retain auditors. What they found was the Lakeview Park lease wasn't the only one that had expired, but none of the others had the kind of impact on the community Lakeview had."

Reese curled his fingers around the cup. "What's to become of Carlos?"

"Temporarily suspended while an investigation is under way."

"What are you not saying, Yvonne?"

She leaned in and lowered her voice. "The council suspects he might have been taking kickbacks. If this is verified and it comes out, the media will have a field day."

"You're right. If you think you've seen angry people now, just wait! This is how riots get started."

Reese took another sip of coffee and eyed Yvonne over the rim of his cup. She'd taken a huge leap of faith telling him this. Why?

"And I take it I'm supposed to keep this information to myself," he said.

"You can use it however you want," she said shrewdly. "All I ask is that my name is kept out of it." Yvonne reached across the table, brushing his knuckles with hers. "I like you a lot, Reese. You're a good man. If something should change between you and Jana, I'll be waiting."

With that she got up and left.

For a long time after her departure, Reese stayed seated, replaying the conversation in his head and coming up with a plan. Then, deciding he had nothing to lose, he retraced his steps, crossing the street again, and headed for the Rothschild building.

It was time to have another conversation with Bruce and maybe this time he would get somewhere.

Chapter 22

"Jana, I'm afraid I'm going to have to ask you to separate yourself from that group," Darlene Harding said, her lips a tight white line. "Your full concentration needs to be on the job you get paid for."

"I volunteer at Lakeview Park," Jana reminded the woman who was her boss. "I use my personal time to provide much-needed services." What she wisely did not say was that considering her puny social worker's salary, her boss was way out of line telling her how to spend her personal time.

So that's what this summons was about. Jana had initially been surprised to receive the message from Darlene that she wanted to speak with her. It was rare that their paths actually crossed, since Darlene did not have an office in the building. Most of their business so far had been conducted via e-mail or phone.

They'd gone back and forth for several days and finally a meeting had been set up. Darlene's position as executive director meant she oversaw a large district running from Del Mar to Ocean Beach. Today was the day she'd agreed to come in.

"What I am most concerned about," Darlene said, regaining Jana's attention, "is all that awful publicity. Your face has been all over the television set. Thankfully, neither your name nor our organization has been mentioned. What about the people you service here? Aren't they to be considered as well? You have a responsible position. People look up to you. How do you expect your clients to take heed of your counsel when you're coming across as a rabble-rouser?"

Darlene's face reminded Jana of an overbaked garlic knot, the kind served with pasta.

"I don't recall picketing in front of Lakeview Park. Nor have I allowed myself to be interviewed by the press," Jana said sharply.

"You're being disrespectful."

"I'm not." Jana shoved to her feet. "Just give it to me straight. Where is this going?"

"I'm putting you on warning. Your job is in jeopardy."

Jana breathed through her mouth. "What is it that I'm not doing? What could I be doing better? I've been with you five years. I've had excellent evaluations and no write ups."

Darlene now rose to her feet as well. She spread her hands across the desk, Jana's desk. "You'll be receiving your first write up today. It will be for absenteeism."

"What! I haven't called in sick once this year."

"But you've left during the work day several times. Those are unauthorized absences. Any organization has a right to expect a certain level of attendance."

"How about this?" Jana countered, her tone deceptively even. "The level of attendance you can now expect is none. I quit. Now please get your feet out of the way so that I can get my purse."

Bending over she yanked open a drawer and removed her purse.

"Aren't you being hasty?" the odious woman sputtered.

"Not in my book. Have a nice life, Darlene!"

"You can't just walk out. You have to give notice."

"I just did," Jana said, sailing by her. "What more notice do you need? I told you I quit."

"I know it was an impulsive thing I did," Jana admitted later when they were seated on Twyla's little backyard patio, a pitcher of sangria separating them.

"You were starting to hate that job anyway. Too many cases and too little money. Now you'll have time to devote to the business."

"Point well taken but meanwhile how do I pay my bills?"

Twyla topped off both glasses before saying, "We did okay at the judge's retirement party and we did more than okay at that bachelor auction. Plus we have the Lakeview Park groundbreaking ceremony and dance coming up. Maybe it's time you took a salary."

Jana felt the pain of regret slice through her. She'd fought a good fight for the citizens of Lakeview Park and there was nothing further she could do.

"I don't know if I would feel right catering and planning an event on a site whose development has caused such consternation," she answered. "I'm surprised the organization would even consider hiring us. I've already been labeled a troublemaker."

"The contract's been signed for quite a while ever since Rhonda Watson, the Rothschild's PR person, contacted me. How would she know you and I are associated? And even if she did why would she care? Her main interest is ensuring the event goes smoothly, meaning food and beverages are out on cue, flowers set in strategic places, and musicians in their places at the appointed time."

"True but people are petty."

What Twyla had proposed was more than feasible. Jana would now have more time to explore more opportunities for A Fare to Remember. The business now had a healthy bank account.

"That's why we're a good balance," Twyla said, sounding a little giddy from having one-too-many glasses of sangria. "On another note, what about this man of yours? I haven't heard much about him lately."

Jana then launched into a long dissertation about men who couldn't be trusted while Twyla continued to sip her drink. Finally Twyla called a halt to it. "Whoa! Have you even talked to the man or heard his side of the story?"

"No. What would be the point? How can I ever trust him again?"

"You're being unfair. He's tried and found guilty in your mind without benefit of testimony."

"How can you say that?" Jana cried, jumping up and almost spilling the pitcher of sangria. "You're my friend, you're supposed to be on my side."

"That's what friends are for—to let you know when you're wrong."

Jana had ignored all of Reese's messages. She just couldn't bring herself to talk to a man who'd known that his people were going to be treated poorly, yet did nothing to stop it.

Why was it that everyone seemed to be taking Reese's side and wanted to give him the benefit of the doubt? Her mother had basically said the same thing as Twyla.

Mona had urged her to give Reese another shot and Jana hadn't followed through.

"What have we been hired to do?" Jana asked, switching the conversation.

Twyla told her what the plans were and although Jana pretended to listen, her thoughts kept returning to Reese. She missed him so much it was almost a physical ache.

Reese stuck his head into the open doorway of Bruce's office. It was after hours and the developer was conducting a one-way conversation with someone on the other end of the telephone while Seth Bloom sat looking amused. Reese carried a rolled-up set of plans under one arm.

"Do it because I say so."

"I'm the one calling the shots, not you . . . If it means employing security officers, undercover or otherwise, then do so. That's what I'm paying you for . . ."

"Don't waste my time with these petty issues."

Bruce then slammed down the phone.

"The guy's a putz. You should replace him," Seth laughingly said, implying that the party on the other end of Bruce's abuse was an idiot.

"He's been with me a long time. Loyalty's got to count for something."

"I suppose."

Reese cleared his throat. That got both men's attention.

"What's up?" Bruce asked, sounding wary.

Seth nodded, barely acknowledging Reese's presence.

"Can I have a word with you in private?"

Bruce narrowed his eyes. "Is this about the Lakeview Park development or something else?"

"It's about the development."

"Then it's nothing that can't be said in front of Seth."

Bloom so far had not shown any signs of removing himself from the picture—if anything, he'd settled more comfortably into his seat.

"This is pretty serious," Reese warned. It was no skin off his nose if Seth Bloom wanted to be witness to this conversation. Reese had thought it through clearly. At this juncture of the game he had nothing to lose and everything to gain.

"Speak up, man." Bruce's attention returned to the paperwork he'd picked up from his desk and was glancing through.

Okay. If that's what he wanted that was what he would get.

"Carlos Pinellas has been suspended," Reese began, looking closely at Bruce for a reaction.

Bruce's jaw muscles twitched. He continued to feign interest in his papers. Seth Bloom was now sitting up straight, his expression guarded.

"Yes, so what does the city manager's suspension have to do with us?" Bruce asked.

Although a monstrous desk separated them, Reese made sure he positioned himself directly in front of Bruce.

"It's come to light there were several leases Carlos allowed to expire. One of those leases is Lakeview Park. There's talk that he's been taking kickbacks."

Another muscle in Bruce's jaw jumped. "So?"

Reese pressed his advantage. "If that's verified, Carlos is in danger of losing his job and may even be facing criminal charges."

"I'm still not sure what that has to do with me," Bruce said, flashing a confident smile before looking to Seth for reassurance.

Reese shot him a smile right back. Two could play the same crafty game. "It has everything to do with you. Which is why I'm here." He was taking a long shot but what the hell. "Carlos's back is to the wall. He's making loud noises that you and a number of other developers paid him big bucks to let these leases expire so you could scoop the properties up for your own gain."

"That's ridiculous."

"I hate to tell you what's going to happen if any of this goes public. It will probably be one of the biggest scandals San Diego has ever seen. Reputations will be ruined and we're talking jail time here. Either way it's going to be an expensive fix. Not to mention the development will be held up again while the situation is being investigated."

"Where did you hear this?" Seth interjected, now looking as if he'd swallowed a golf ball.

"Oh, I have my sources."

One of Bruce's fingers worried an eyebrow. "Everyone in this town knows that Pinella's a drunk. No one's going to believe a word he says."

"I'm not so sure I agree with you," Reese said, leaning in and setting down the plans. He splayed both hands across Bruce's desk. "Drunk or not, he's the city manager. What reason would he have to conveniently allow several leases to lapse?"

"Maybe he's just incompetent," Seth offered.

"According to Horace Lakatos he called Carlos's office many, many times and left messages. If a landowner, especially one with Lakatos's clout, is calling, that should have jolted a memory or two. Incompetent or not, you would think Carlos would return one of those calls or at least make the association a lease might be coming due." Reese paused, his fingers now stroking his chin. "Unless Carlos was benefiting in a major way from these lapses of memory."

Bruce shot out of his chair. "And just what are you implying?"

"I'm not implying a thing other than what Carlos himself has stated. And I'll say this again: Word gets out and there will be repercussions. Riots in the streets. Think Detroit, think Newark, and think LA. Not pretty. Are you willing to have your organization's name ruined? I'm not sure I'm willing to put my reputation on the line."

Bruce had turned an ominous shade of crimson, and Seth looked like the golf ball was in danger of being expelled from the closest orifice.

"Whose side are you on anyway?" Bruce demanded.

"Your side, of course. I'm counting on you to be a hero. Which is why I am asking you to approve the revised plans on your desk. I've come up with designs for both affordable and middle-income housing. And I've added the fishing piers back, along with plans for a brand new community center with a much more upscale look."

"But . . ." Bruce said, openmouthed.

Reese inclined his head. "So I'll be expecting to hear from you, gentlemen. Now, there's a personal matter requiring my attention."

Chapter 23

Two days later, Reese stood in front of Jana's apartment. He took a deep breath and rehearsed again and again just what he was going to say. It was the second, or maybe it was the third time he'd come by. So far, pressing the buzzer had yielded no results. Determined to try again, he pushed longer and harder on the bell than he'd planned to.

What was up with the woman? His phone calls and messages had not been returned.

Placing a finger on the buzzer, he pressed again. He could swear he heard movement behind the closed door, and Jana's red pickup truck was parked in the spot out front. Why was she playing games?

"I know you're in there," he yelled, loudly enough for the neighbors to hear. "You might as well let me in. I'm not leaving."

The front door flew open and Reese came face-to-face with an apparition from the *Amos 'n Andy Show*, whiteface and all: Winston, wearing face cream, and a do-rag tied Aunt Jemima-style, filled the doorway, blocking his progress.

"What do you want?"

The greeting was rude enough to let him know he was not welcome. Reese wondered if Winston's coldness had anything to do with the length of time he'd pressed on that buzzer, or if Winston had been sent out to get rid of him. If nothing else Jana's roommate was loyal.

"I'm looking for Jana," Reese said politely. "How are you ,Winston?"

"Feeling like crapola now that you're here. Jana's not in."

Reese drew himself up to his full height of six foot two and raised an eyebrow. "Her truck's parked outside. Is she running?"

"Probably from you. She's not here, boyfriend. And even if she is, she doesn't want to see you."

Winston attempted to close the door. Reese stuck his foot into the opening.

"I'm not going anywhere until Jana speaks with me. If she doesn't want to see me, she'll have to tell me that to my face." Gently nudging a surprised Winston aside, Reese entered the apartment.

"Jaaanaaa!" he shouted, making it sound like Brando's "Stella!" in *A Streetcar Named Desire*.

"I told you the woman isn't home," Winston said, now doing a series of stretches, bends, and gyrations, his neck bobbing, like Michael Jackson used to in his moon-walking days. "Twyla came by and picked her up."

"When will she be back?" Reese persisted.

"How the hell am I supposed to know? I'm not her keeper. Since you forced your way into our home, might as well plant your butt in front of the TV. I sure as hell am not entertaining you. I've got things to do."

Winston did another pirouette before disappearing.

Reese was left to plant himself on the couch and watch a soundless television.

He must have fallen asleep because the next thing he knew a hand was on his shoulder and a shrill voice in his ear.

"What are you doing in my home?"

Reese tried to focus on the vision in front of him. He could smell the honey of Jana's skin. Even the hostility in Jana's voice sounded sexy to him. He ran his hands over eyes that felt gritty. "I came to see you, baby. You weren't returning my calls. Pretty cowardly I'd say."

"Puh-leese." Jana swatted the air, dismissing him. "What if I'm just not interested in taking things further?"

"Didn't appear that way to me the last night we were together," Reese said slyly.

That seemed to stop her midstream. Jana's lower jaw became unhinged, flapping uselessly, then she rallied.

"You have a lot of nerve. Don't tell me you didn't know Rothschild had plans to lock those poor people out. You were pretending to be interested in me, when what you really wanted was to pick my brain so you could run back to that unscrupulous mogul and tell him those poor people's next move. You'd do anything to get that information, even sleep with me."

"Aren't you being a bit irrational?"

Reese ducked as a papier mâché clown, the type you can buy in Mexico, went whizzing by his head. He was wide-awake now.

Behind a closed door he heard Winston titter.

"Irrational nothing. You used me. You don't give a crap about our people," Jana shouted back.

So that was what this was all about. She felt used and that he had let her down. He began to protest.

"Don't you say another word," Jana said, rushing over to the television and turning up the volume.

Bruce Rothschild's face filled the screen. A reporter bellowed a question so fast Reese missed it, then shoved a microphone under Bruce's nose.

"We ended our association immediately," Bruce said, staring earnestly into the camera lens. "The Rothschild organization has never condoned inappropriate or illegal behavior. We did not know Seth Bloom was engaged in illicit activity."

"But he was your vice president of acquisitions," the reporter shot back.

"That he was, and I trusted him implicitly."

"And you had no idea he was accepting bribes…?"

"None at all. I'll have to refer you to my legal counsel…"

"What about kickbacks? It's been rumored Bloom paid people off on behalf of your organization. Take for example the lease associated with Lakeview Park—"

"Speaking of which," Bruce's face creased into a wide smile. He'd obviously been well coached. "Lakeview Park's groundbreaking ceremony is scheduled in two weeks." Bruce looked around as if expecting someone to appear. "Where is my urban designer when I need him?" he asked, grinning from ear to ear. "This is big. I mean really huge." He paused for effect. "Picture fishing piers open to the public, a grand new community center bigger and better than the current one, indoor and outdoor olympic-sized pools…affordable restaurants, and free mental health counseling for those that need it."

"What!" Reese heard Jana's sharp intake of breath directly behind him. She turned to Reese. "How did you pull this off?"

"I didn't," he said modestly. "Bruce is no fool. He knew he needed to do something quickly to regain public support for this project. It's simply a strategic move."

"But he was so against a community center," Jana said with shiny eyes. "You heard him. He wanted to get rid of a 'certain element.'"

"And in many ways he will. If by 'certain element' he means drug dealers and pushers. The building and surrounding land will probably have more security than you know what to do with running around. But sorry to say, it's not going to be built on the original site, but in the midst of all those affordable homes."

"You're the one who made it happen," Jana said, hurling herself at him and flinging her arms around his neck.

"Someone had to design those plans, baby."

"And that someone was you," she said, kissing him soundly on the mouth. "You dirty, rotten liar."

Reese kissed her back, shutting her up for a moment, he hoped.

A door slammed less than discretely behind them.

"Excuse me."

Winston. Oh well, Winston would just have to make himself scarce.

Every aching bone missed this woman. Somewhere along the way Jana Davis had wormed her way into his heart and worn down his resistance. Commitment still scared Reese, but not as much as it scared him not to have this woman in his life. He wasn't willing to take that risk.

Behind him a reporter droned on. Reese barely heard something about Carlos Pinellas resigning before he bent his head and kissed Jana again.

When he surfaced, he prudently said, "Come home with me, baby."

"I think I will."

Two weeks later, under a beautiful California midday sun, ground was broken on the New Lakeview Park, or "The New Lake View," as the media now called it.

The news of the occasion had been all the buzz, and it had brought out an eclectic crowd. Dignitaries in expensive suits and well-shod feet were mingling with people of every age and ethnicity. There were the requisite hangers-on and cronies who normally came to these events, along with the San Diego elite.

Champagne and wine were circulating as if they were water. Heaping platters of hors d'oeuvres were now being served under colorful tents draped in tulle and cabbage roses. Lucy, her new boyfriend, Roberto, and their friends were the waiters and waitresses. On the grounds, silver- and gold-coated fairies and elves roamed, handing out balloons and chocolate kisses to children and adults alike.

The atmosphere was festive and fun. This was a new beginning for Lakeview Park.

Twyla and Jana had coined the event "The Lakesummer Dream," and as such they'd let their imaginations take over.

Mayor Sapperstein had already made his long, drawn-out speech. Then Rhonda Watson had introduced Bruce Rothschild. The real estate mogul was now busy pumping hands with the same people he'd locked out a few weeks ago.

Jana couldn't help thinking how quickly things had changed.

"Isn't that Bruce Rothschild heading our way with

your man in tow?" Twyla asked suddenly out of the side of her mouth, elbowing Jana in the side.

Jana snorted. "What does he want?" She meant Bruce.

"I guess we'll see. We've received nothing other than compliments so far and we've already secured five jobs."

Jana felt a momentary twinge of apprehension. Bruce must be stopping by to complain about something. He'd pretty much ignored their existence at the function up until now. He'd been too busy puffing out his chest, accepting congratulations and bragging about how wonderful the finished product would be.

Now Jana wondered if the drinks were too watered down. Was the shrimp undercooked, the chicken curry too hot? Had one of the papier-mâché sprites floating on the tent's ceilings become disconnected from its tether, and clonked some VIP on the head?

"My, your man is turned out," Twyla mumbled out of the side of her mouth again. "He's wearing Armani if I were to hazard a guess."

"Shush. They're almost on top of us."

Jana smoothed the peplum of the sundress her mother had practically forced her to buy that evening at Neiman's. She ran her fingers through her smart new haircut, wishing she had time to glance in a mirror. As of yesterday, the blond curls were no more. She'd had the stylist change the color to an attractive shade of auburn. Would Reese like her new look?

Bruce and Reese were only a few feet away.

"Ladies, you've outdone yourselves," Bruce brayed, pumping first Twyla's hand, then Jana's. "I was saying to Reese that we should keep you on retainer for all our upcoming events."

Twyla smiled brightly, her calculator of a brain assessing the profits. "That would be nice."

Jana wasn't so sure how nice that would be. She didn't trust Bruce Rothschild one iota, but money was money and he still maintained a lofty reputation. No charges had been levied against him. He'd gotten off scot-free. Seth Bloom had been the fall guy.

"Nice hair," Reese said, reaching over and winding a strand of the newly auburn hair around his finger.

"Think you can handle another job?" Bruce boomed, his voice making several heads turn.

"That depends," Jana said diplomatically.

"How'd you like to head up the human services division of my new community center? You'd have carte blanche to hire the number of social workers you'll need. Betcha anything, my pay is better than anything you could get off the street."

Obnoxious ass. Jana shot Reese a look. His eyebrows arched slightly. She knew him well enough by now to know what he was thinking. There hadn't been a night they'd spent apart since he'd arrived at her door uninvited. Winston was now busy advertising for a roommate.

"How about I get back to you?" Jana asked. "You might have a policy about relatives in your employ."

She flashed her left ring finger at him. An emerald, big enough to cause a serious black eye, sparkled. It was surrounded by baguettes.

"You two are engaged?" Rothschild actually seemed shocked. "You don't waste time." He nudged Reese. "Congratulations."

Reese took Jana's hand, swinging it back and forth as if they were children at a playground. "This is the woman I've been waiting for my whole life. I'm hungry, baby. Let's see what you can feed me. 'Bye, Bruce."

Leaving Bruce behind to continue the conversation with Twyla, they began walking toward one of the larger tents.

"Did you see his face when you walked away?" Jana asked when they were out of earshot.

"Who cares? I've completed my designs and I've gotten the bulk of my pay." He patted his pocket. "Any additional services associated with this project will be billed separately." He kissed her ear. "By the way, baby, over my dead body will you work for that man."

"Now, now," Jana said. "Let's not be hasty. Putting A Fare to Remember on retainer isn't a bad deal. It's not exactly working for the man. Think about it. You're an independent contractor. Rothschild offers you a lucrative job—you take it or leave it. That's just the way the game is played."

Reese kissed her cheek. "You're quite the little operator, my love."

"Learning from the best, darling. Learning from the best."

Inches away from the tent, while people streamed by them, Reese stopped her.

"Jana Davis, did I tell you how much I love you?" He brought her hand to his cheek.

Jana stared into eyes that reminded her of a soothing after-dinner liqueur. She stuck the tip of her finger in the dimple on his cheek. "Only about a hundred times since you came over to my apartment, then dragged me off to your place."

"Then I'll tell you again. I love you, Jana Davis. Everything about you. Even your uh . . ."

"Don't say it."

"Exotic taste in clothes. Do you love me?" He sounded boyish and uncertain.

"Well, I don't know. You're arrogant and proper. Some might even say anal-retentive. Your habits will probably drive me crazy. But baby, no way am I throwing you back. So yes, I love you just the way you are," she sang. "Now ditch the tie and let's eat."

Reese loosened the knot on his tie and surprised her by slipping it around her head and tying it seventies-style. "Now you look more like the woman I first met." Then he dipped his head and kissed her.

The world went still as Jana floated on a comfortable cloud. Lakeview Park and its community of warm, wonderful people were left behind as she gave into the feeling of belonging to this man.

Reese McDonald had been a custom design. From the very beginning her parents knew it, even if she didn't.

Now she wondered why it had taken her so long to realize it. She and Reese were a perfect fit.

Always had been.